DO NOT REMOVE
CARDS FROM POCKET

CROOKED FLIGHT

BASIL JACKSON

CROOKED FLIGHT

St. Martin's Press
New York

Library of Congress Cataloging in Publication Data

Jackson, Basil, 1920-
   Crooked flight.

   I. Title.
PR9199.3.J37C7   1985   813'.54   84-22258
ISBN 0-312-17650-3

First published in Great Britain by Robert Hale Limited.

First U.S. Edition

10 9 8 7 6 5 4 3 2 1

ONE

The Learjet touched down on the single-runway airfield at 2:30 p.m. Marshall was waiting outside the wooden flight shed, his stubby figure hunched forward expectantly.

"There's a four-wheel-drive jeep outside," he said as we shook hands. He hurried toward the small parking lot.

"Who's on your Go-Team?" I asked as we climbed into the vehicle and drove off.

"Bill Houston and –"

"Covered in oil as usual." I grinned.

"Best engine man in the business," he growled. "And Liss of course."

"Probably Downey, too?"

He nodded.

"You know how to wangle the best guys on to your team."

His lips parted in an uncertain smile as he glanced at me over the tops of his glasses. "That's why I called you." With a spade-ended gnarled fingertip he twirled a tuft of hair poking from his ear.

We drove on for several miles in silence. He would open up when the time was right. Now it was to his advantage to hold back, letting me into the know gradually, sucking me into the job by enticing my interest with little dollops of information released at calculated intervals to arouse my curiosity. Crafty old buzzard: he knew my weakness. And my

5

strength – that's why he'd called. We turned off at an intersection where a signpost pointed to Whistling River Falls.

"Crazy placename," I remarked.

"That's Wisconsin," he said drily. A half-mile farther on he added, "Lived in this state as a kid. Great for fishing."

We changed direction again, and started climbing a narrow forest road. On both sides tall trees rose like cliffs.

"Rough country," he commented.

We made another turn. The vehicle bumped over a gravel road. After a quarter-mile of bone-rattling ride he leaned toward me. "It was a Novajet."

He slowed the jeep, made a ninety-degree turn, and we lurched forward. After a mile he turned to me again.

"At flight level four-one-zero when it last reported."

He stared into the dark trees ahead.

"Gave his flight level and repeated his next reporting waypoint. Detroit."

I gave an interested nod.

"Didn't get to speak to Detroit." He shrugged. "Didn't enter their control sector."

He peered ahead again.

"Madison saw his blip vanish. They couldn't raise him again. A logger phoned to say a plane had crashed in a logged-out area."

"No other radio contact after he reported to Madison?"

"Absolute silence."

That surprised me. "All the way down? No cuss words? Screams? A Mayday?"

He looked at me with the intent eyes I had known so well. "Nothing."

"How many aboard?"

"Four. Two pilots. Two passengers."

"And of course – "

He shook his head. "Slammed in vertically. Bill worked out the trajectory."

He braked, and turned into a path bulldozed between trees. A couple of hundred yards farther on we drove up a rough logging road, the engine roaring. The debris of logging operations – wet split ends of huge tree branches, smashed bark – lay on the uneven path. The wheels slithered on damp ground.

We came out of the forest at last into a clearing where stumps of trees remained. As usual, my stomach rolled over at first view of the crash site. The pulverized hunks of aluminium and steel debris were scattered in a wide circle around a crater. We stopped before a cordoned-off area and climbed from the jeep. Shards of twisted metal, tangles of battered fuel and hydraulic pipes, and festoons of electric cables lay everywhere.

I looked around. "No fire."

Two investigators in coveralls crouched over a dark shape that had been hurled against a tree stump. We walked towards them, avoiding bits of metal. I recognized Houston's form, his big belly bulging under scruffy coveralls. He was bending over the remains of one of the engines. He thrust his arm into the guts of the machinery and twisted.

"Hand me an oil sample container," he said to the man at his side. He took the glass jar, inserted it into the engine, and withdrew it filled with oil.

"Get this off to the labs right away. Get 'em to do a spectrometric analysis for metallic particles."

The man screwed the lid on the container and hurried to the helicopter parked at the edge of the clearing.

A grin of recognition lit up Houston's face. "Hi – Doyle." He wiped his hands on a rag and slapped my shoulder. "Good to see you." He turned toward the wreckage.

"Mighty fishy one, this."

"Why?"

He looked at Marshall. I got the impression he wanted approval to talk about what they'd discovered in the debris, all that remained of a twin-engine executive jet that had slammed in from six and a half miles up.

"Wait until Doyle's looked around," Marshall said. I got the feeling he either wanted me to discover something for myself or was purposely delaying telling me something important. Another psychological ploy. Transparent.

"Have you found everybody?" I asked.

"The two passengers. Not the pilots yet."

We picked our way over the bits of riveted metal and jagged edges of ribs that looked like wing components. A lifting hoist had been erected over the crater, and mounds of woody earth had built up as the men below threw up shovelfuls of soil. A couple of men stood by with green-black plastic body bags. I wanted to move on, but Marshall and Houston showed no inclination. This was one reason why I'd given up eleven years of air-accident investigation. The work of putting together the parts of the puzzle fascinated me: still did, but the gore ultimately got to me. The shattered, bloodied human carcasses had made me a casualty. I watched the digging men for a few seconds and turned away abruptly.

I stomped toward the trailer that had been set up on site to serve as a field office of operations. Glancing back, I saw Marshall look up, nudge Houston, and set off after me.

We sat around the table in the trailer. Houston poured coffee. I sipped in silence, staring at the warm liquid, feeling it unfreeze the block of ice where my guts should be. The battle within me vacillated back and forth. I looked up at Marshall.

"When did it happen?" I asked.

"Three days ago. In daylight. Madison Air Traffic Control can't pinpoint it exactly because the logger who phoned had to walk out through a forest trail to base camp. He estimated that took about twenty minutes."

I wanted to know the rest: what was the weather? Who was aboard? Where was the aircraft going? Purpose of the flight? The standard questions. But then my mind retreated, see-sawed, and I wondered why Marshall had called me long-distance with such urgency last night. I glanced up. His eyes were waiting. I motioned toward the notebook at his elbow. He opened it and read:

"About 11:30 Central Standard Time on May 9, a Novajet, registration number N23456J, crashed in a logged-out area 2.5 miles southwest of Whistling River Falls, Wisconsin. The aircraft had contacted Madison Air Traffic Control, giving a flight level of four-one-zero. ATC instructed the pilot to repeat his flight level to Detroit ATC as the aircraft approached Detroit's sector. Madison ATC reported the aircraft blip disappeared from the screen but was unable to make contact with the aircraft. Approximately twenty minutes later a witness called to say that an aircraft had crashed."

Marshall glanced up, adjusted his bifocals, and continued.

"The weather was CAVU. Surface winds at Madison were southwest at eight knots. Ground temperature sixty-two degrees Fahrenheit."

A rare and mysterious crash. Nosedive from cruising flight. Weather: ceiling and visibility unlimited.

"The aircraft left San Francisco at 0235 Pacific Time. Destination: J.F.K. International, New York. Estimated time of arrival at JFK was 1735 Eastern Standard Time."

He looked up and saw the question on my face.

"No refuelling stop. The aircraft was fitted with long-range wingtip tanks."

I nodded.

"We've checked ATC. The pilot reported at all the scheduled waypoints. The flight proceeded, up to that point, exactly as planned."

"And the purpose of the flight?" I asked. Houston shot a glance at Marshall. There was a long pause.

"A mystery?" I asked.

The tension reacted on my shoulder: my right arm was acting up again. I pulled the helpless limb closer to my side. Marshall grasped his notes, and flipped the page.

"The aircraft was registered in the name of Ling International Import-Export Corporation, of San Jose, California. Privately-owned by that company."

"Have you recovered the Aircraft Journey Log?"

"It's in a hell of a state, but legible. In the safe."

He indicated the safe built into the trailer side for storing critical evidence. "Lists the passengers' names, too. Unusual. Pilot was Captain Don Phillips, forty-one. First Officer was Edward Warnett, thirty-four. The two passengers: Gunther Nordsen and Angelica Oraschuk."

The roar of an engine rumbled across the clearing. In a moment the flumph-flumph of a helicopter's rotor sounded. Houston's oil sample and other bits of evidence off to the test labs in Washington.

"The entry for the flight was scrupulously filled in. Gives the amount of fuel loaded – including the long-range wing-tip tanks of course – time take-off permission given, and the usual other information."

I hugged my arm. Caution told me to hang back: curiosity propelled me forward.

"Was a CVR installed?" I asked. Contained in a crashproof steel case, the Cockpit Voice Recorder, which taped the conversation in the cockpit, would produce concrete evidence.

"No. Neither was there a Flight Recorder," Marshall replied. Lines of disappointment deepened around his mouth. Such a recorder would have provided data showing in what positions the flight controls and engine settings were at the moment of crisis.

"The aircraft was not equipped, nor was it required to be equipped, with Cockpit Voice Recorders or Flight Data Recorders," I said, quoting the air accident regulations manual from memory. They were not legally required for privately-owned aircraft.

A hopeful smile passed across Marshall's mouth. He and Houston exchanged glances.

"There was no explosion, no fire and – no witnesses," he went on, playing on my interest.

"What about the logger?" I was weakening.

"He saw the aircraft diving from a distance. Heard the crash. Didn't actually witness the pile-in."

"How far away was he?"

"Half-mile, estimated."

"Not much use." But you can't expect witnesses out in the middle of nowhere, I reflected. Airplanes don't suddenly drop out of the sky on cruising flight from forty-one thousand feet. On a CAVU day. Most accidents, statistics showed, occurred on landing. Nearly one-third.

I thought about the subject I hated. "Are you going to do lactates on the –er, the crew when you find them?"

Lactate profiles, a medical procedure, to determine who was flying the aircraft, was a relatively new process. Traces of more than normal lactate acid were present in tensed muscles, such as thumbs and fingers gripping controls.

"No need. It was on auto-pilot," Marshall said. As I had expected.

"You've confirmed it?"

"Auto-pilot switch was in On position. Jeff Liss opened

up the mechanism. It was in operating mode."

Marshall leaned forward and steepled his huge hands under his chin, looking like a judge but, incongruously, a judge expecting a verdict rather than giving one. The decision was up to me. Houston burped, and noisily helped himself to another sandwich from the kitchen counter. Then Marshall looked me directly in the eyes and said in a deliberate voice, "The plane ran out of fuel."

"Would you mind repeating that? I'm not sure I heard right."

"The plane crashed because it ran out of fuel."

"It had long-range tanks," I countered. "The log shows all tanks were topped up at San Francisco. The Novajet with long-range tanks can fly coast-to-coast without refuelling."

"We've been over it a hundred times with the lab people. It *was* fuel shortage." He ran his fingers through the white fuzz on top of his head. "Christ – I know it sounds unconvincing when stacked against the hard facts of fuel tank capacity, the consumption figures of the engines, the aircraft's speed – everything logical. But –" he hammered the table with a mighty fist, spilling Houston's brimming coffee mug – "the goddamned plane had simultaneous flameouts on both engines because it ran out of fuel."

Houston grabbed a napkin and soaked up the spill. "We opened up the internal wing tanks. Dry as nuts."

"And the wingtip tanks?" I asked.

"Sheared off on impact. Landed in trees. Empty too. Although there were patches of fuel seepage under the trees where we found them."

"That's significant."

He shook his head. "Bit of residual fuel left after the pilot switched to the internal wing tanks."

"And no explosion, no fire," Marshall affirmed. "Nothing to burn."

My arm twitched. I rubbed my shoulder. Now it was clear why I'd been aroused from bed. Marshall had come up against a solid wall. Anything to do with fuel systems, fuel instruments, flowmeters, gauges, booster pumps, filtration, transfer valves, cross-over valves – anything that got fuel from tanks to engine combustion chambers – in the old days was referred to me. I was supposed to be the fuel plumbing expert. This was the second time I'd been called to help in two years. I was becoming a sort of consultant emeritus.

"Where did you find the turbine blades?" I asked, leaning forward. It was a standard question: when jets crashed with engines running at cruising revs the turbine blades, like the blades of a revolving fan, flew off due to centrifugal force, and came to rest a long way from the crash scene. Blades of an engine that stopped in flight didn't fly off when the plane crashed, because the turbine wasn't revolving. That is, if the plane piled in from a relatively low height. On the other hand, turbines could windmill fast if engines stopped in flight and the plane plunged from a great height. The air rushed through the engine, causing a windmilling effect. So one had to be careful when viewing the evidence.

"More than six hundred feet away," Houston said.

"Then why your conclusion?" I challenged. "The engines were likely windmilling all the way down."

"Bill just told you," Marshall said, a bit stuffily. "The tanks were dry. Except for seepage from the wingtip tanks."

"But hell – airplanes don't usually run out of fuel."

"I know that, for Christ's sake," he replied testily.

"Upper headwinds? Upper level jetstreams?" I said as a final challenge. It was a method of hammering out and nailing down facts. The way we used to. Like a court of law: facts based on solid evidence, with a prosecuting and defending counsel. Judgment came, after weeks, often months, of painstaking investigation when the investigator-in-charge took a sheet of paper and started to write what the consensus of the many parties considered the cause or probable cause, of the accident. It was a summation of opinions gathered from his Go-Team, the aircraft and engine manufacturers, the airline, the Air Line Pilots' Association, the Federal Aviation Administration and other so-called "interested parties".

Marshall shook his head. Signs of impatience showed: fingers drumming the table edge, a quick movement of the eye.

"There was no unforecast weather. I've checked Met and ATC over the entire route."

"Fuel gauges?"

"For Christ's sake, Doyle. You know gauges are unreliable evidence. The fuel gauges were at zero."

Fuel gauges were sometimes at zero when a plane crashed. But that didn't mean the aircraft had run out of fuel. Modern gauges were electronic and when electric power shut off at the moment of impact, the digital readout zipped back to zero – sometimes. I'd seen some odd cases. In a crash dive, with the aircraft vertical, fuel sloshed to the downward end of tanks and the gauges played funny games. I'd been at crash sites where the gauges showed Full but the tanks had been near empty.

"What about the crossfeed valves?" I asked.

"Bill and I took them to pieces. When the engines cut the pilot tried feeding extra fuel from the left tanks to the right engine, in an attempt to get one engine re-started." He shrugged. "Didn't work."

"You seem sure it was fuel shortage," I reiterated.

Houston answered. "Empty fuel lines." He put down his mug and shook his head. "How can a plane loaded to the gunwales with fuel run out of the stuff?" he asked, his moustache working. "The logs shows *all* tanks were topped up at Frisco."

"You've checked the ground services there?"

"Of course," Marshall replied, huffily. He saw the indecision that must have been etched on my face. Then he slowly got up, crossed to the safe, and opened it. Houston shot me a dark glance. Marshall hefted out a battered steel box the size of a shoe box and placed it on the table. Crumbs of earth clinging to the box fell on his notebook.

"We found this yesterday," he said with an overtone of mystery, trying to prise off the lid of the box with a kitchen knife. "It came off easily –"

"Try this," Houston said, producing a heavy screwdriver.

Marshall inserted the blade between the lid and the body of the box. He levered off the lid. I peered inside. My eyebrows shot up.

"You found this in the crash?"

"Yes," he said, watching my reaction.

I looked at the contents for several moments in silence. "Well – what's surprising about that?" I said at length. "Electronic microchips. So what?"

"Look at this one – and this," he declared, offering a selection of the tiny components from the palm of his hand.

I picked up the pea-sized parts. "*Military* microchips," I exclaimed, inspecting the MIL specification numbers on the wired-on tags.

"They sure ain't Pac-Man chips," Houston muttered.

"What were they doing in a civilian private jet that crashed in the wilds of Wisconsin?"

"That," Marshall said with a jubilant edge to his voice, "is another reason why I called you." He smiled. "I know you like playing the other kind of detective."

I scooped up a handful of chips from among the thousands in the box. "This load must be worth several hundred thousand dollars."

"More'n a million bucks," Houston asserted. "I knew a guy in the business."

"It depends on what the chips are for," I said, moistening a fingertip and putting it on a chip the size of a grain of sand. It stuck to my skin. "I heard some of these can store more than sixty thousand bits of computer information."

"And those," said Marshall grimly, "can store *military* information."

I examined the box. Although distorted, it had survived the crash well. I lifted it up and inspected the bottom.

"What's this?" I indicated wood splinters stuck to the bottom.

"The box, apparently," Houston said, "was hidden in a wooden crate."

"Hidden?"

"Yes – hidden," Marshall asserted.

"Nothing criminal about that. They were probably going to tranship it elsewhere," I said.

Houston grinned secretively as he refilled his mug.

"The crate," Marshall explained, "was approximately five feet by three feet by two feet high. Bill and I made a re-construction from the bits of smashed wood."

I admitted to myself that that put a different light on it. "How did they get such a big crate into a Novajet?" I asked.

"We assume they must have removed two of the six passenger seats. Bradley's trying to put together the seat wreckage to confirm it."

There was a long silence, except for Houston's slurping.

I said doubtfully, "*Perhaps* they were concealing the box. But why?"

"You're in air chartering." There was a glint of mischief in Marshall's eyes. "What's *your* guess?"

"I haven't any guesses today. Only a hunch –"

"What the hell's the difference?" Houston interjected.

I smiled. "A guess is based on imagination. A hunch is instinct."

"What does that mean?" Marshall demanded.

"You know as well as I do. They intended to trans-ship the thing overseas."

"Smuggling?" Marshall seemed to want confirmation of his own suspicion.

"Dirty word. Dangerous, too." I leaned back. "Found address labels? Customs Declarations?"

He shook his head. "The crate was completely smashed. But we found these."

He went to the safe and came back with an armful of colourful plastic toys: miniature model cars; a tiny fire truck; bulldozer; railway engine.

I laughed. "And when you find the Customs Declaration form you'll know what'll be written on it.' They used these for packing."

Marshall seemed pleased. I knew that he knew he was leading me closer to accepting the job, but somehow the microchips and these toys had altered things: I was more than usually curious.

"You gotta admit they're ideal," Houston said, picking up a toy sports car and scooting it across the table as he made vrooming noises. "My kids would appreciate this." He crushed it between an oily thumb and forefinger and released the pressure. "See how it bounces back into shape."

I picked up the roadster and squeezed it. Ideal for shock absorption. Pliable. And light-weight.

I examined several other toys. "These are only the shells. An electric motor goes here, with a battery there. See this bracket?"

"Yeah," Houston said. "Hadn't noticed."

"They may come with electronic controls too – with

microchips," I suggested.

Marshall was openly smiling now as he saw my interest. "Seems logical," he agreed.

"Maybe the guys who made these," Houston went on, flipping over the toy railway engine, "are connected with chip-making."

"But which came first? Do they make chips only and buy the toys; or make toys and buy the chips?"

"*Military* chips," Marshall reminded me.

"I told you we thought the crash was fishy," Houston said.

I looked over the microchips and the little toys.

"You'll have to report all this to the FBI. In accordance with the regulations."

"Of course," Marshall said. "But I wanted you to see the stuff before they took it away."

"There's a heavy penalty for smuggling. I know an air cargo handler who nearly became an innocent victim."

"What happened?" Houston asked.

"He accepted a shipment, a crate, for delivery to Frankfurt, West Germany. The Customs Declaration and other paperwork showed it contained industrial electronic equipment. It actually concealed a stolen highly-sensitive microwave surveillance receiver capable of picking up transmissions from United States' spy satellites and from our embassies abroad. You can guess where it would have gone from Frankfurt."

"What happened to this guy you know?" Houston asked.

"Luckily an FBI agent visited him before his aircraft took off – the crate was already aboard. The agent explained that the receiver was on Uncle Sam's munitions list as an espionage item – not to be allowed outside the United States."

"I had no idea you had problems like that in your

business," Marshall said.

"I don't. I'm in air chartering – not air cargoing."

"Oh – I forgot."

"I do a bit of cargoing on the side, to help a client out. Nothing major."

I held out my coffee mug. Houston grabbed the pot. As I sipped in silence I could see *the* question framing itself on Marshall's face. I got up, walked the length of the trailer, and flung open the door. A knot of investigators were gathered near a hoist erected over the crater, pulling a chain through well-oiled pulleys. They were lifting a huge mass of pulverized metal. It looked like the aircraft's nose section – a smashed nosewheel rim was cemented into the metal. Others farther off sifted through the outlying debris. Two men had set up a tripod and were photographing bits of components that had been flung from the crater. The photos would be used to construct the wreckage distribution chart that would be a permanent pictorial record after the relevant bits of rubbish had been carted back to the laboratories in Washington.

I shut the door and stood facing it. The decision wasn't something I could delay – it had to be made *now*. I felt Marshall's eyes on my back. I swung around.

"If you get the fuel system components to the labs I'll come," I said.

He got up and shook my hand. "Thanks," he said simply.

"Glad to be working with you again," Houston said.

I took out my notebook. "I'll jot down the numbers of some of the chips."

There were a lot of round gold-coloured chips with MIL-Z-0007 tags wired to them. They stood out because of their colour and size. Massive for a single-unit chip: big as a fingertip. They appeared to be integrated into micro-circuitry embedded in the plastic. They looked complex.

"Are you heading back to Seattle now?" Marshall asked.

I nodded. "Can you arrange for the Learjet to take me back to Chicago? I'll catch a regular flight to the Coast."

I'd get Pender, my general manager of operations, to take over. Business wasn't soaring: the recession had forced big industrial clients to cut back on air chartering, ordering executives to travel by scheduled airlines. Times were tough.

I stared at the microchips, strange gems in a scarred jewel box. Then I thought of Nordsen and the woman passenger.

"I wonder where she fits into all this. *Cherchez la femme?*" I said.

"What the hell does that mean?" Houston asked.

"Search for the woman in the case," Marshall explained. "Didn't you go to school?"

"Night school," Houston replied, a big grin on his face.

TWO

The librarian was helpful, but talkative. After she'd made a list of a dozen trade associations and discussed the possibilities of finding Ling Intercontinental Import-Export Corporation in each, I caught her in mid-breath and blurted, "I'll try the Directory of American Importers and Exporters first. That may be –"

"You must check out the Index of American Manufacturers also," she interrupted. "Some manufacturers export *and* import."

She peered at me through granny glasses balanced on the tip of her nose. I got the impression that she thought people who walked into the Seattle Main Library Reference Section *had* to be dunderheads. She handed me a list of numbers she had compiled. I obediently took the long slip: when I was alone in the stacks I'd check only the more relevant ones.

"Thank you. You've been most helpful," I said.

"I'll show you where the correct stacks are," she insisted. No escape.

She led me between the high shelves, treading between students sitting cross-legged on the floor and elderly gentlemen squinting sideways at titles.

"Start here," she ordered, sliding her hand reverently along the spines of several thick volumes. "I'll be back in a minute to see how you're making out. Oh – I forgot. You must check the History of Import-Export Control Orders released last month by a Senate sub-committee." I sighed. "I'll look up the Dewey catalogue number. Back in a moment."

She sashayed down the narrow aisle. When she disappeared I scanned the volumes, grabbed the Directory of American Importers and Exporters, and ducked between a gap in the stacks. Too late. She reappeared at the head of the aisle, waving another slip. I froze, clutching the big tome in my good hand, feeling like a one-handed thief caught in the act. She rushed up.

"Stack 33A. Top shelf – "

"Yes – thank you –"

"Call me if you need anything else. I'll check again to see how you're getting on."

I slunk into a little clearing where students sat at tables. There was one vacant chair. The heavy book slipped and thudded on the table.

"Shh-shh –" A woman grimaced.

"Sorry."

I scanned the Li's. There were scores of Lin's, and Lines and Lincolns and Lindburgs but only three Lings: two in Chicago and one in New York. I re-checked. No Ling with a registered head office in San Francisco. I tapped my fingertips impatiently on the table.

"Shh-shh."

What to do? A swishing sound at my side, and the young woman appeared.

"Here's some more," she whispered, placing another list before me.

When she'd gone I checked the Index of American Manufacturers. I plodded through hundreds of pages, diligently followed the cross-indexing and – found a bold-face listing for Ling International Import-Export

Corporation. Head office address; San Jose. Click-click: the area from San Jose to San Mateo was Silicon Valley, where existed the biggest concentration of electron microchip manufacturers in the world. Under the Ling listing: plastic toys, games, playthings, school supplies and miscellaneous. Directors: G. Nordsen, president; W.O. Beech, vice president, engineering; A.R. Oraschuk, secretary-treasurer. I scribbled the names and titles in my notebook and lugged the books back to the shelves.

She bustled toward me, carrying yet another list.

"You must check these."

"I found what I wanted. Thank –"

"Oh." She seemed disappointed.

I eventually escaped, jumped into my car, and headed for the General Aviation section at Sea-Tac airport. After telling Pender what had happened, I ordered the little Cessna to be wheeled out, gassed up, and flew down to San Jose. Inside forty minutes I braked a rented Hertz in front of a small concrete building in the outskirts. A buxom fair-haired woman about thirtyish sat typing behind a desk in the tiny entrance lobby. She was strategically placed near a closed inner door. She didn't look up as I entered, but persistently searched for the keys and pecked hesitantly. I thought: receptionist pinch-hitting as a typist.

She ponderously finished typing a word before looking up with cold, suspicious eyes. I handed her my old National Transportation Safety Bureau business card on which I'd inked in my home phone number.

"I'm helping with the investigation of the crash of your company plane," I said truthfully. "I'd like to see Mr. Beech."

She stiffened. Her jaw dropped. She studied the card, clutching it between scarlet talons.

"Do you have an appointment?" she asked guardedly.

"No –" My arm twitched. I'd got off to a bad start.

"Mr. Beech only sees visitors by appointment." Her voice had a raspy edge. She turned to the typewriter as if dismissing a supplicant who'd asked for a donation for the Home for the Deaf.

"It's urgent. I must see Mr. Beech."

"Mr. Beech will not be in today."

"When will he be in?"

She hesitated between pecks at the keyboard.

"I can't say."

"But do you *know*?"

Her head jerked up, eyes flashing.

"No," she snapped, tearing the paper from the typewriter. She stood up and turned to the closed door. "If you'll phone next week, perhaps Mr. Beech will be in."

"Is there someone else I can see – the general manager? I have only a few questions. About the plane's operation."

"Mr. Beech is the only person with authority to speak on behalf of the company." Her voice had a German or Scandinavian accent. I wasn't sure.

"*When* Mr. Beech returns, will you please give him my card?"

She seemed relieved that I was leaving. "Yes, Mr. Trimboli."

I pretended to turn, but suddenly swivelled toward her. "I'm sorry about Mr. Nordsen and Miss Oraschuk –" It might have been *Mrs.* Oraschuk for all I knew.

She clutched the sheet of paper against her body. All colour seeped from her face.

"Are you all right?" I asked.

She closed her eyes. "Yes –" she whispered.

Then she recovered, opened the door and stepped through, shutting it quickly before I could see beyond.

* * *

I discovered where Beech lived by looking up the street directory. But there was no telephone number listed, and the telephone book didn't give it. A check with the operator confirmed that he had an unlisted number. An hour after leaving the Ling plant I drove slowly past Beech's house. It was a white stucco building with a terracotta roof that peeked from over the top of a high wall completely surrounding the property. I had a glimpse through iron grille gates of a triple garage with closed doors, and a dash of lawn. I parked the car a hundred yards beyond and walked back. The gates were locked together with a heavy chain and double padlocked. There was a button in a panel on the gatepost. I pressed it.

"Who's there?" It was a young male voice from a speaker set in the gatepost.

"My name's Trimboli, Doyle Trimboli. I wish to see Mr. Beech. Is he there please?"

"Dad's not home."

"When do you expect him?"

A long silence.

"When do you expect your Dad home?"

"Just a minute," the voice said.

There was the sound of a presence moving away from the microphone; another voice, a woman's, in the background.

"Who is this?" a woman asked suspiciously.

I told her. "It's important that I see Mr. Beech. I'm an aircraft-accident investigator. Is this Mrs. Beech?"

"Yes," she said hesitantly. "Aircraft accident –?"

"Your husband's company plane crashed in Wisconsin."

There was a long silence.

"My husband," she asked in a thin voice. "Is he –?"

"He wasn't aboard."

Another silence. Traffic moving on the road behind me made listening difficult.

"Was – anybody – hurt?"

She genuinely sounded as if she hadn't heard. I told her what I knew, and included the fact that the four people aboard were killed.

"Oh – my God," she cried shrilly. "Who – who was –?"

"Mr. Gunther Nordsen and an Angelica Oraschuk."

She sucked in her breath.

"– and the two pilots."

Silence.

"Mrs. Beech? Are you still there?"

"I – I didn't know. Wilbur didn't tell me about it before he went off – away on business."

"When do you expect him back, Mrs. Beech? It's impc₁tant that I speak to him about the plane." I stabbed in the dark. "I understand he was responsible for the aircraft's operation."

"I can't discuss my husband's –"

A mover's truck roared along the street. The sound cut her off. When it had gone I said, "Mrs. Beech, will you please allow me to come in to speak with you?"

A long silence. A buzz sounded in the speaker. An electric lock clinked in the gate.

"Mrs. Beech. The gates are padlocked."

Two or three minutes passed. Then a lad about eighteen appeared on the path. He was powerfully built, and walked awkwardly, leerily, toward me. His sour face was plastered with acne.

"Hi," I said.

He didn't reply, but inserted keys in the padlocks, twisted, and opened one of the gates wide enough for me to slip through. He looked up and down the street and quickly re-locked the chain.

"Why the high security?" I asked.

He stared down at the path. "I dunno."

Mrs. Beech was hidden behind the door as she swung it open a crack. She let us in, and glanced outside before locking it.

"Why the high security?" I repeated. "San Jose isn't famous for its high rate of break-ins." I had no idea what the statistics were.

"When did the plane crash?" she asked, ignoring my question.

"Tuesday afternoon."

She began to weep, holding a handkerchief to her eyes. She was a thin, shrewish woman, with dull hair that betrayed lack of care. The story was easy to see: Beech the successful executive, vice-president of a manufacturing company in hi-tech industry, flying about the country in the company's jet. I glanced about. Rich household and a failed marriage. The boy, who had silently slipped away, was a victim of the mismatch. Did Nordsen fit into the picture? And the secretary-treasurer?

"Please – sit down," she said. "I haven't heard anything. Nobody's called me. Poor Phyllis. Has someone told her?"

"Who's Phyllis?"

"Gunther's – Mr. Nordsen's wife." She sobbed heavily. "They've only been married a year."

"I don't know if she's been informed, Mrs. Beech. I can only assume next-of-kin were notified by the police."

That was the usual procedure: it wasn't NTSB's job. Their responsibility ended when identification was confirmed. I wondered about that. Marshall had recovered the passengers' bodies, but the pilots' had still been in the process of digging out when I was on site. That was yesterday. He'd probably confirmed all names by now.

She turned her head from side to side in a motion of denial, crying uncontrollably. Her distress found a crevice in my armour, and I stared into the empty fireplace. I was again at the controls of the little airplane I had designed and built. It had taken hundreds of weekends, interrupted from time to time by telephone calls to dash to the site of various Majors. When the Certificate of Airworthiness arrived, I made a solo flight, did some adjustments to a pesky aileron control and made several other test flights.

"Daddy – Daddy – take us for a ride," nine-year-old Anne clamoured.

I strapped her in alongside her kid brother Peter. Sarah sat next to me. The aircraft behaved like a dainty ballerina. I kept her steady and level at six thousand, made a ten mile circle and approached the field. It happened on final. The engine cut at the last minute. I pressed the starter and worked the throttle. The airspeed indicator sped down the clock. I steadied her for a deadstick landing. But the left wing unaccountably tipped. I shoved the control column full over to correct, but too late. The wing tip hit the ground and we plunged in. Four years later I haven't got used to living alone. And my goddamned right arm –

Mrs. Beech took a deep breath and stopped crying. I looked up from the fireplace.

"Forgive me," she said in a reedy voice. She looked scared.

"When do you expect your husband to return?"

She bit her lip. "I don't know. Sometimes he's away for four or six weeks at a time."

"Is something –" I broke off abruptly.

"What's that?"

"I was wondering if –. You look, er, bothered."

She grasped her hands in her lap. Tears sprang into her eyes again. "It's awful. So awful." Then she pulled herself together and said, "Tell me what happened to the plane, Mr. Trimboli."

I gave her the general picture. "It was *en route* from San

Francisco to New York – "

"New York?"

"That was the filed flight plan. New York."

She fell into one of those silent lapses that I was beginning to think were part of her personality. Forced upon her by a domineering husband. I wondered what he looked like, and glanced around the room. There were no family pictures.

"Why does that surprise you?" I asked.

"It doesn't," she lied.

"Mrs. Beech. As special investigator with the National Transportation Safety Board I am authorized to ask questions that give clues why this aircraft crashed." It was my turn to lie: "Questions that go beyond the usual range of our investigation."

I let it sink in.

"We have reason to suspect that the aircraft was carrying a cargo of an unauthorized nature," I went on. I thought of mentioning we suspected intent to smuggle out of the country, but decided against it. Too early.

Her eyes widened. A gleam shone beyond the tears.

"Huh –" she broke off.

"What's that?"

"Nothing."

She pushed away a dangling hank of hair, a movement that emphasized her unattractive appearance. She wore a grey woollen dress that hung on her bony figure like a shapeless rag on a puppet. She had flat saucer-shaped breasts and a nothing waist. In a word: unsexy.

"Mrs. Beech. Why are you surprised the plane was going to New York?" I put a measure of demand in my voice.

"My husband usually flies to the Far East. He's in –" She averted her eyes. "My husband's in Tokyo right now."

"I don't understand. Your husband, fortunately, wasn't aboard the company plane. What has the fact that he's in

Tokyo got to do with your surprise that the plane was going to New York?"

"I – I guess I'm confused. The shock –"

I didn't believe her. Had she *wished* her husband had been aboard the company plane?

"Mr. Beech won't be back for four or more weeks?" I affirmed.

"Sometimes he stays three months at a time. Especially in Tokyo."

"You didn't say that before. Is there some place I can contact him by telephone?"

"Never tells me what hotel he stays at. Moves around. On business, you understand."

"Is there anyone else I may talk with at the company who can answer questions about the plane's operations? A general manager, perhaps?"

"My husband, besides being vice-president, is also general manager and is responsible for the plane's operations. It's only a small company, Mr. Trimboli."

But rich enough to own and operate a million-and-a-half-dollar Novajet. I made one more try.

"We need to see the aircraft's official papers – the maintenance records and other documents. Have you any idea where they are kept? And who I see to get a look at them?"

"My husband keeps official papers like that."

"Where are the papers?"

She seemed to rally again. "Frankly, Mr. Trimboli, I don't know." She rose suddenly. "And what's more, I don't damn well care." She dried her eyes and turned to go.

The youth, who had reappeared, scowling still, let me out of the door. I gave a backward glance: a skinny, used-up woman tossed aside by an ambitious husband, wealth, prestige and financial success. As I followed the lad down the path I tried to imagine the beginning: the pretty bride; eager, handsome groom; well-wishers; confetti; limousines; flowers. The kid unlocked the gates. I drove the rented car back to the airport and climbed into the cabin of my old Cessna that Pender had nicknamed *Holy Ghost*, and flew it back to Seattle.

When I got to my apartment I was hungry. I'd always been a good cook, even before I married, and decided to warm up the roast I'd left in the fridge. I put it on a slow heat, and to make sure it was done to perfection, jabbed the electric meat probe into it to more precisely control the oven temperature; the probe had a wire that plugged into the oven-heat control. While that was taking care of itself, I made a chef's salad and boiled potatoes, and thought about the missing Mr. Beech.

Then, when everything was done, I set a place for one at the dining-table, propped the *Seattle Intelligencer* against the wine bottle, and forgot about the events of my day.

THREE

Al Goodwin had been in air cargoing since I'd known him, which was twelve years. We'd met at the forced-landing site of his first aircraft, an ancient DC-3 that was heavily mortgaged to the bank. I'd been IIC, sent from the regional office. Goodwin had been piloting, and had made a skilful landing in scrubland after encountering navigational difficulties that had resulted in his running out of fuel. He had obstinately believed that the plane was salvageable, despite my contrary opinion. He rebuilt the underside of the fuselage, repaired the wings, and ordered a new undercarriage from McDonnell-Douglas. The thing passed its FAA airworthy tests six weeks after the crash and subsequently made enough money through air cargoing for Goodwin to look his bank manager in the eye.

"Cigar?" he offered in his corner office at San Francisco International. Through the windows I could see the tall buildings of downtown.

"Don't smoke, thanks. Wouldn't mind coffee."

He spoke into the phone and swung his feet up on the windowsill. A taxiing DC-8 caught his attention.

"Special order." He nodded toward the plane as he replaced the receiver. "Herd of dairy cows to Paris." He grinned, "Sixty cows for some bull's harem."

"Pity the guys at the other end. Cleaning up –"

"We installed special trays." He watched the DC-8 roll

into take-off position. "Paid the last cent on that old baby last month."

"You've come a long way since the bailiffs nearly grabbed the DC-3."

"Ha –" He took a cigar, bit off the end, stuck it in his mouth and flicked a lighter. "What can I do for you?"

Before I could answer a young man entered with coffee things. I waited for him to leave.

"You told me a yarn about how you got caught smuggling stolen electronic gear out of the country. Military equipment. But you were innocent."

The cigar jutted upward as his jaws worked. "I was goddamned lucky. They could have clamped me behind bars. I *was* innocent."

The roar of a jet taking off rolled across the airport and rattled the windows.

"You're chairman of a new committee in the Air Cargo Carriers Association. An inquiry. About how easily cargo carriers become innocent victims of smugglers."

He looked surprised, but didn't ask how I knew.

"I wasn't the only guy suckered in. Turns out half the membership had similar experiences." He pulled the cigar from his mouth. "Hey – you haven't been conned?" he added, concern in his voice.

I shook my head. "Nothing like that. I charter aircraft, remember. And don't fly overseas."

He tapped ash into the tray on his desk. "Why are you interested?"

I told him I'd been called in by the NTSB as special consultant on a crash. And that some suspect cargo had been found in the wreckage. "What you tell me will be treated with the strictest confidence," I emphasized.

"What sort of suspect cargo?" he asked, eyeing me shrewdly.

"Military electronic components."

"What type?" His direct questions reversed the roles. I swore to myself.

"In confidence?"

"Yes."

"Electronic microchips –"

He straightened. His eyes filled with interest. "That's something I know about. There's a hell of a lot of microchip theft – and smuggling. Our committee went into it deeply. We contacted the FBI and they briefed us."

I pulled my chair closer. "How do they do it?"

"Smuggling? Crate a load of chips, make out a Customs Declaration form saying it contains electronic components – even be honest and declare they're electronic microchips – and phone us, or any air cargo handler, and we ship it overseas."

"You don't have to specify what type of chips?"

"No." He paused. "Customs men aren't technically qualified to know the difference between a Pac-Man chip and a guided-missile chip. A Pac-Man chip may go into the electronic guts of a nuclear submarine's navigation guidance system, or into a fighter plane. Some serve the same function."

"The military chips found in the plane wreckage could be civilian chips used for military applications?"

"Yes." He mashed the unfinished cigar in the tray.

"Not likely. They had MIL – that stands for military – specification tags wired to them. In a privately-owned, civilian plane. What's Customs doing to beef up their regulations? To protect guys like you."

"Making an attempt. But it's useless. Smuggling's linked to theft. And while Customs tries to keep tabs on what's coming into the country, the Department of Commerce tries to develop trade between other countries and the United

States. They work against each other. You heard about the leak of American high-tech knowhow to countries behind the Iron Curtain?"

I nodded.

"All connected. When a customer phones me to pick up a shipment to fly to Zurich, or Milan, or West Germany, I don't know if the stuff's secret military high-tech equipment that will end up in Moscow or Prague." He reached for another cigar. "I've got no protection."

"The Pentagon has the Munitions List. For items that mustn't leave the United States. Super-secret equipment."

He nodded. "There's another list called the Commodities List. Administered by the Department of Commerce. See what I mean? The branches of government duplicate red tape. Work against each other." He shook his head. "And dopes like me get crimped in the middle."

"Where does the FBI come in?"

"Espionage – counterfeiting. Ha – another crimper."

"They got you off the hook on that receiver thing you nearly smuggled out."

"They grilled me for twenty-four hours. I could have got two years in jail, and a one-hundred-thousand buck fine. That would have bankrupted Goodwin's Air Cargo Service."

He turned to a file cabinet. "You're a curious devil. That first time we met."

"My mother told me to peek under carpets. I questioned you pretty hard." I smiled, and poured another coffee.

"Here're some case histories. You're welcome to take a look. They're confidential so –"

"Of course."

I browsed through the file, surprised at the number of cargo handlers named. Some were big organizations; others small firms struggling on the border line of bankruptcy. I made a few notes and handed the file back.

"Use your phone?" I asked.

"Go right ahead."

"Long distance. I'll make it collect."

Marshall answered. He sounded relieved. "Been trying your line all morning."

"I'm in San Francisco. Got all the fuel components ready?"

"No. I've been trying to reach you to tell you that one of the bodies isn't the body we thought it was."

"Oh –"

"The body we expected to be Angelica Oraschuk's isn't her's."

"Whose is it?"

"Wish we knew. It's so badly mangled even Downey can't identify it. The other pathologists are equally baffled."

"So how do you know it's not the person you named?"

"It's a *man's* body."

When I recovered I said, "Is the other passenger the one we thought?"

"Yes. The pathologists agree. Nordsen had an amputated pinkie finger – lost it in a car accident. And his dentist confirms identification through plate impressions."

"So who's the other passenger?"

"We don't know."

Beech? I thought madly. Why would Nordsen and his vice-president both fly to New York with a hidden box of military microchips? And why would Angelica Oraschuk's name be entered in the Aircraft Journey Log if she wasn't aboard? If Beech was alive, and in Japan, where was Oraschuk? Did they know what was concealed in the crate? They could have been transporting it for someone else. Keep it in mind.

"Have you found the Customs forms or address labels?"

"Still looking," Marshall replied. "A hell of a job. You saw how the debris was scattered. Got everybody looking now. And I'll check Customs' records."

I told him something about microchip smuggling. He seemed impressed.

"We know the airlines do it unknowingly. The scheduled's have complained to the International Civil Aviation Organization, but not much has happened."

After I put down the phone I thanked Goodwin, and he arranged for a car to drive me to where I'd parked *Holy Ghost*. The refuelling serviceman had neatly laid out the pilot's seat belt ready for buckling up. On the dashboard was the credit card receipt. I put it in the glove compartment and noticed that someone had stuck a paper slip from a Chinese fortune cookie on the back of the plastic door. Probably one of Pender's mechanics.

Try new beginnings. They often lead to success.

FOUR

The new beginning turned out to be something different from what I had in mind, which was to discover precisely what business Ling International Import-Export Corporation was engaged in. Marshall called to say that ninety percent of the Novajet's fuel system had been recovered and was ready for re-assembly in the labs. I caught the early morning scheduled from Sea-Tac and was in Washington by late afternoon.

I dropped by Marshall's office, and together we went along to the lab. Turney, the director, was standing outside his office, giving instructions to a couple of technicians. He greeted me in the off-handed manner that had been so familiar. I had always had the impression he'd never liked me, and the feeling came across now. As usual, he wore a frayed sweater and hang-loose corduroy pants, and his hair was untidy. His carrot-shaped face still had that life-is-a-misery expression that I had known on an almost daily basis.

"I've set it up over there," he muttered, indicating a workbench at the far end of the room. He went back into his office.

The Wreckage Analysis Laboratory wasn't a big room. It didn't have to be because only components of aircraft were tested in it: large-scale re-assembly of crashed aircraft, if this procedure was considered necessary by the IIC, was usually done at the nearest airport to a crash site.

The bent and squashed fuel pipes had been straightened and clipped to a vertical board erected on the bench, following the outlines of blue and red chalk lines. Various fuel system components – pumps, filters and electrically-operated valves – were lined up on the bench for my inspection. Nearby were the two battered engines, on wooden stands.

"Where are the cockpit fuel contents gauges?" I asked.

"In the instrument setup over there," Marshall replied. "You want to see them?"

"Yes – later." I considered them part of the fuel system, not merely as instrumentation.

Turney joined us, bringing a stack of blueprints. He spread one, entitled Fuel System Schematic, on the bench.

"We didn't get everything, as you can see," he said. "But I don't think the missing bits are critical."

I checked the schematic, and agreed. Putting a work glove on my left hand, I picked up a pump, and inspected the card tag wired to it. An investigator at the crash site had scribbled *From Right-Hand Wing-Tip Tank*.

"You've taken this to pieces?"

Turney nodded. "And tested it on the rig."

"And?" He had an annoying habit of leaving out details.

"Checks out A-Okay."

I picked up another pump. It was tagged *Left-Hand Wing-Tip Tank*. Called booster pumps, they were bolted inside the long range tanks, immersed in the fuel, and were electrically-operated. They pushed fuel through pipes to the engines where other pumps took over.

I spun the shaft. It jammed. "Shaft's bent."

"Impact damage," Marshall said. "Bill found it. Mounting bolts sheared off on impact."

Small components such as pumps, valves and even cockpit instruments sometimes suffered only minor damage even in catastrophic crashes. But it was essential to differentiate between component damage due to in-flight failure, and damage due to crash impact.

"We must take it to pieces," I said.

Marshall smiled. He seemed relieved that I was double-checking his own investigation. It was accepted practice in the Board's work to get a fresh pair of eyes looking at stuff hauled back from a crash site. And that, I reflected, was why Marshall had called me.

I selected a wrench and undid the securing nuts while he held the pump. The top lifted off. In a few seconds I had the tiny fan-shaped impellor in my hand. I sighted along the shaft.

"Like a bent elbow. Got a magnifying glass?"

Turney fished in his pocket and handed me a glass. There were no strain lines on the shaft indicating that a side load had been applied.

"You've checked for fatigue?"

"Yes."

I stared at his pimply face. "And?"

He walked to his office and returned with a selection of blown-up photographs. Marshall leaned over as I sifted through them.

"No beach marks," I said, peering through the magnifying glass.

Metal fatigue showed on photographs as barely detectable wavy lines. We called them beach marks because they looked like the wavy lines left on a sandy beach when the tide went out.

"Let's keep in mind the possibility of slipshod maintenance treatment," I added. A mechanic may have dropped the pump when he re-installed it after a major overhaul of the aircraft: I'd check the Overhaul and Repair Schedule. Normally, fuel tank pumps were not removed once installed at the factory, but on some aircraft types the maintenance manual called for bench-testing the pump, to make sure the pressure output was up to requirements.

"The manual doesn't call for bench-testing at overhaul," Turney said, voicing my thoughts.

I made a mental note to check the manual. Then I turned to the valves on the bench.

"Four crossover valves. What does the Flight Operations Handbook say about the procedure?"

Marshall took a black-bound book from his attaché case. He flipped the pages. "Fuel management system," he said, jabbing a fingertip on the page. On the facing page was a fold-out coloured diagram of the complete fuel system.

"Complicated for a twin-engine plane." I read the instructions for the crew.

"Usual procedure. Take off on the main internal tanks and switch to the wing-tip long-range tanks. Burn off that fuel first."

They nodded.

"Rely a lot on electrical controls," I added, pointing to the lines representing wires on the diagram.

"We thought so too," Marshall said. "Bill and I did a check-up on the electrical power supply."

"In case of power failure in flight," Turney commented redundantly.

"No circuit breakers were off," Marshall said. "Nothing that would suggest in-flight power failure. Anti-collision strobe lights switches were on at impact. And there was power to the cockpit instrument lights."

Investigators were trained to check electric power sources early in an inquiry. And there was a way to tell which lights were on. Hot filaments rarely snapped when an aircraft impacted, because they were flexible; cold filaments in unlit lamps, on the other hand, were brittle. They snapped. The rule sometimes applied even when lamp glass envelopes were smashed.

I looked at the other components spread on the bench, and turned to the lab director. "Where's the fuel system management panel?"

Turney lifted a plastic sheet.

I studied the switches on the panel. "Damned complicated."

"I sure wouldn't have designed it that way," Marshall said. "Too much switchery."

"Where did the panel fit in the cockpit?"

"On the pedestal between the pilots' flight instrument panels."

"So either pilot could operate the switches."

I turned the metal panel over. "Surprisingly little damage."

"We found it jammed against the nosewheel tyre. Cushioned the shock," Marshall said.

I checked the switch settings for cruising flight, and compared them with the Flight Operating Handbook. Switches for the wing-tip tanks were in Off position; those for the main tanks, inside the wings, were On.

"Everything fits," I said. "What's this red warning light?"

"See page fifty-six," Marshall said.

"If the fuel pressure's lost, the light comes on. Did it?"

"Filament smashed to hell," Marshall growled.

"They didn't have to depend on it. There's a fuel-pressure gauge right here." I pointed to the fuel management panel.

"You know what it's like. Taking things for granted in the cockpit."

Recent research had shown that the more flying hours a pilot accumulated, the more prone he was to accepting as routine the tasks of cockpit drills. In cruising flight, with the tension of take-off eased, an unconscious feeling of relief took over. There was always the temptation to believe all was functioning normally, and little things sometimes were not given the attention they should be. As a leading aviation medico had put it at the Dulles school when I was an investigator-in-training: routine is the enemy of flight safety. But routine in the form of easier-to-read electronic instruments on the flight deck was being promoted by engineers as aircraft became more complex. It was an irony of the modern era of flying machines that the more complex they became, engineers specializing in what they called "machine-man interfacing" designed more complicated instruments with more parts to go wrong.

I turned to the fuel filters. There were four, each the size of a large ketchup bottle. I opened them up, examined the elements.

"No blockages."

"The crossover valves fit here," Marshall said, pointing to gaps in the piping system clipped to the board.

Crossover valves and their associated pipes enabled a crew to feed fuel to a left-hand engine from the right wing tanks, or a right-hand engine from the left wing tanks. It was a safety feature designed into all multi-engined aircraft. I picked up a valve and checked the position of the interior mechanism.

"He was feeding all remaining fuel into the right-hand engine."

I imagined the scare in the cockpit when both engines stopped: the steady, reassuring hum gone, the shock when they realized it was fuel starvation, the anxious checking of the fuel management panel, puzzlement that the red warning light indicating low pressure hadn't lit up, the hurried crosschecking of the pressure gauge and the contradictory evidence of the instruments. And then action: flipping cross-over valve switches, directing fuel from the left wing internal tank to the right-hand engine – as well as from the right wing internal tank, to drive every drop of the precious liquid into one engine – to regain at least fifty percent power. The realization that even that was impossible. The attempt to regain control when the airspeed abruptly ran down the scale and the aircraft began dropping through space. Even if they'd regained control the angle of glide of a sophisticated plane such as a Novajet would be too steep for them to have glided for a deadstick landing at Madison. Everything had happened too quickly.

I turned to the battered engines. "Is Bill around?"

Marshall picked up a phone. "Be right along."

He appeared a few moments later, stuffing a hot dog into his mouth. Even when not in baggy field coveralls Houston looked huge. His belly overhung his belt; he had a chest and head that seemed to topple his body, and he walked with an out-thrust neck.

"Hi, Doyle. Didn't expect to see you again so soon." He stared at the crumpled things on the bench. "Any clues among this lot?" He squeezed mustard from a plastic package onto the remains of the hot dog before popping it into his mouth.

I shook my head and pointed at the engines. "Got time to go over the engine fuel system with me?"

"Sure – sure. Where shall we start?"

Marshall excused himself: "I've got a meeting with the Board." He looked sombre.

"On this case?" I asked.

"No – the Miami mid-air."

Thank God I'm not involved, I thought. It had been horrendous. Two four-engine high-density-seat aircraft: seven-hundred and fifty-seven dead; no survivors. In a moment of lost self-control I was back on site of my last Major. It had been an Arrowaire that had crashed in Texas, one of the new twin-engine wide-bodied airliners recently introduced into airline service. A long parade of men were carrying pine coffins toward a huge tent that had been erected at the crash site, others scrambling with stretchers over the rough terrain, with green plastic body bags bobbing on the stretchers as the men picked their way through the metallic rubble, still smoking although the crash had occurred two days ago. The pathologists inside the barn, wearing respirators – it was July and the temperature in Florida was in the high nineties – trying to identify bits of flesh and crunched human remains.

"Another negative," the pathologist's voice was muffled as he turned to the man following with a clipboard. He pointed to one of the waiting coffin bearers. The crisped remains were carefully lifted, placed in the coffin, and borne to waiting trucks outside.

My eyes re-focused on Houston as he poured a coffee from the urn that always stood in Turney's lab.

"Let's start at the fuel filter," I said mechanically.

"Take this one," he said, turning to the nearest engine.

We took the filter apart again; he had previously done it. Then we traced the internal fuel passages to the barometric control valve and, ultimately, into the combustion chambers.

Another memory bore in: I was in the identification tent on site, the place where the civil authorities directed relatives of the dead passengers. I had been in the tent looking for Houston, where he'd gone to speak to Downey, the Go-Team pathologist in charge of the Human Factors Section. A woman had come to identify the remains of her husband and two children.

"Do you recognize any of these as belonging to your

husband or –?" a morgue attendant asked. He indicated a table where personal objects were laid out for inspection: a gold marriage ring; a burned necktie; battered dental plates; a ripped shoe.

The woman had stood at a distance, unable to bring herself to approach the table, peering from behind the corner of a handkerchief held to her face. She shook her head. When the attendant held up a fragment of a teenager's denim jacket, she fainted.

Houston said, "Clean as if it had just come off the assembly line."

We went through the procedure for the right-hand engine. The combustion chambers were wrecked, but the internal piping, and the flexible lines, were in good shape.

"Let's pull off the pumps," I said.

We took our time: a philosophy installed in trainees at the air-accident investigation school at Dulles International. The engine-driven fuel pump on the right-hand engine had torn from the gearbox, and was damaged. The pump on the left-hand engine was in good shape. We unbolted it and took it apart. I spun the shaft.

"Moves freely. Bearings okay," I said.

"The seals are perfect."

"Where to now?" Houston asked as Turney reappeared.

"The fuel gauges. Have you inspected them?" I asked.

"No," Turney replied, "I left them for you."

He indicated a bench where instruments lay under a transparent plastic sheet. The airspeed indicators, altimeters, and engine gauges were badly damaged.

"Doesn't look good," Houston remarked, indicating the smashed glasses on the fuel-gauge windows. The figures showed zero on both gauges.

"Let's open them up," I said.

We did that. Or rather, I did, because I was supposed to

be the fuel-system expert. Houston offered me coffee, but I declined. I used a set of watchmaker's screwdrivers that Turney supplied, and laid out the parts on a sheet of white paper. I inspected the electrical connections, still with bits of wire attached, that led to sensors built into the fuel tanks: the sensors signalled the gauges how much fuel was in the tanks. The connections were solid. Then I examined the tiny array of cogwheels that turned over the digital readout figures.

"Look," I said. They were jammed tight.

Houston slurped coffee and grunted. "What d'yer expect after it slammed into the ground at more than three hundred miles an hour? I worked out the terminal velocity when I did the trajectory analysis –"

I picked up the other gauge. "Another zero."

"Yeah – and you'll probably find the innards as zero as the readout."

"You're a pessimist."

I got busy with the miniature screwdrivers. It took some time: I had never got used to working as a southpaw.

"Surprise," I exclaimed, spinning the cogwheels. The numerals zipped up the readout window.

"Glad I didn't place a bet." Houston grinned.

"We'll have to do a calibration test."

The lab director scratched his head. "What'll that prove?" he demanded petulantly.

"Isn't it obvious?" I asked.

He stared at me with cold eyes. "It'll only indicate how much fuel is in the tank."

Surely he can't be that dense. But I had to make allowances: as chief of the Wreckage Analysis Laboratory he usually had several crash investigations going on simultaneously. Can't expect him to keep track of the subtle investigative points of all of them. But why does he have to be so goddamned touchy? And unfriendly.

"I want a test run. To check fuel consumption compared with flight time. Calibration test with a *new* airplane. Like the test we did two years ago on a *Super Eagle*."

Little signals of resistance flew up in his face. He scratched his pointed chin and turned his eyes away.,

"H'm – very irregular."

"But essential," I insisted.

He locked arms defensively across his shabby sweater.

"What'll it prove?"

"It won't prove anything," I said, a trifle testily. "I want it done to confirm the fuel burn-off rate. See if it agrees with the notations the first officer passed to the captain *en route*."

Marshall's diggers had found several standard paper forms used by the first officer to figure out the fuel burn-off rate as the plane proceeded on its flight path.

He screwed up his lips, worried a pimple with a dirty fingernail.

"It'll take time to rig up," he complained. "But – oh, all right. I'll see what I can do."

He swung around and moved away.

"Nothing's changed around here," I said in a low voice.

"Haven't you heard?" Houston asked.

"What?"

"He's dying. Cancer."

I felt sick. And guilty. I stared after Turney as he shuffled toward his glass-fronted office.

"Does he have a family?"

"Three teenage kids. Wife killed two years ago. Automobile accident."

"Christ –." I paused. "Where's that coffee?"

We stood with our backs to the bench, staring at the engine wrecks. I took a few sips of the insipid coffee and put the mug down.

"Tested for bird ingestion?" I asked, simply for something to say.

It was a standard question. Birds don't fly at 41,000 feet, but in air-accident investigation every question was asked. And re-asked. I'd read that migrating bird flocks had been radar-tracked at altitudes up to twenty thousand feet: for air-breathing animals that was a surprising accomplishment.

"Been over the blades with a microscope," Houston replied. "Negative."

There wasn't much left of birds, even big birds such as geese and ducks, that rammed through the innards of a hot jet engine rotating at speeds in excess of ten thousand revs a minute. Nevertheless, every compressor and turbine blade had to be examined under a high-powered microscope for telltale smears of organic matter – a speck of congealed or baked blood; a quill splinter lodged in an internal air passage; the tiniest fragment of bone or flesh tissue.

Turney came out of his office and walked towards a group of technicians doing a retracting test on an undercarriage rig. He spoke to the man who appeared to be in charge.

"That's the test on the *Star Prober* undercart," Houston said, answering my unasked question.

"Liss told me about it. Undercarriage collapsed on landing at San Francisco."

"Messy business. Killed fourteen. They got me to test the hydraulic pumps. Some clobber-headed mechanic topped up the hydraulic reservoir with fluid of the wrong specification. Rotted the seals. Stuff leaked and the pressure sagged. Theory is when the plane touched down the downlocks collapsed and the kite belly-landed. There'd be no warning horn under the circumstances."

"Warning lights?"

Houston shrugged. "Opinion around here is that the

crew was too busy watching the landing. Gusting fifty-knot crosswind. Torrential rain.''

"There was a committee that wanted to standardize hydraulic fluid specs.''

"It folded. Decided it can't be done. Too many special applications. Design engineers insist on different specs for different jobs.''

"Like the oil specs for your car. They seem to bring in new ones every year.''

Turney approached. "We'll try to set it up later this week.''

"Thank you very much.'' I had no heart to insist on a more specific time. "I appreciate that.''

He slouched away. I turned back to the fuel management panel and regarded it without thought. A telephone rang in Turney's office. He waved at me and held the receiver high.

It was Marshall. Was I ready to accompany him and Houston over to FBI headquarters? They wanted a meeting with us.

I'd never been inside the Pennsylvania Avenue building. Not even on a public tour when I worked in Washington. When Peter was seven he'd bugged me many times to take him. As we entered the hallway my stomach contracted. More guilt. Life is cyclical: the past goes, but returns. Life is wheels within wheels ascending a linear slope. Guilt strikes unexpectedly, riding the circumference of a wheel meshing with a wheel from the past.

"You okay?" Houston asked as I lagged.

"Yes – taking it all in.''

"You look overawed.''

"Cop shops give me the creeps.''

There were two of them and three of us: Houston, as assistant to Marshall, had come as an observer. The boss

man, although the shorter, stood out as Authority.
Gilbertson, for that was his name, looked as if he might have
been a former Army colonel: taut body covered in a
business suit that he wore as a uniform – all jacket buttons
done up even when he sat at the conference table. Wiry
moustache, grey hair brushed sideways to cover a balding
crown. His colleague, Dawson, was skeletal and loosely at
ease. They stared at me as Marshall referred to "the leading
aircraft fuel-system specialist. Called in as consultant." He
added a few words about my background as an IIC and how
my expertise in aircraft air-accident investigation extended
to general detective work. Gilbertson's eyes sharpened their
interest. He looked down at the papers squared in front
of him.

"Mr. Marshall, will you please bring us up to date in your
investigation?" he said. It was an order, not a request.

Marshall did. He concluded: "Everything confirms that
the aircraft ran out of fuel."

There was a long silence. Authority screwed up his lips
and looked sceptical. Bony stared at his papers. I wondered
if they suspected the chips were to be smuggled out of the
country. Marshall did, and so did I. I also had to bear in
mind the possibility of sabotage: it was something every IIC
was taught not to overlook, however remote the idea might
seem.

Authority suddenly jerked his head in my direction.

"How far along is *your* investigation?" he demanded.

I told him.

He let a half-minute go by without comment.

"Do you suspect sabotage?"

"We mustn't overlook the possibility, sir. It's a question
of tracing the fuel –"

"Not interested in the technical crap. Your gut feeling."

"We can't rule it out."

He jotted in his notebook. The possibility of sabotage was now official. I had an impulse to laugh. Houston caught my glance. His eyelash descended in the slightest wink.

Marshall turned to me. "You really believe that?"

I shrugged. "I hope the test I've set up will –"

"How long will that take?" Authority demanded.

"Hard to say. It involves simulating the fuel system management on the flight from take-off to the moment the engines cut."

"Sounds complicated."

"It is."

"I don't want to rush you," said Authority in a kinder tone. "But obviously, we want to know as soon as possible why the aircraft crashed." He looked at Marshall. "If it's sabotage we may assume it's related to the cargo."

"Until such time as our investigation and all necessary tests are completed," Marshall growled, "we can only say at this stage that the cause of the crash remains unknown." It could have come word for word from the Manual of Aircraft Crash Investigation.

Authority cleared his throat. "I understand – I understand." He turned to his skinny companion. "I didn't explain. Mr. Dawson is from the Pentagon. Special Investigations Branch. He's here to tell you the vital necessity of determining the cause of the crash as quickly as possible."

The atmosphere suddenly sharpened.

"The microchips you discovered are listed *Top Secret* by Defense," Bony said in a surprisingly deep voice for so thin a man. He looked from Marshall to Houston. "I understand you gentlemen are security-cleared to *Top Secret* but –" His eyes came to rest on me.

"As consultant to the Board, Mr. Trimboli is cleared to *Top Secret*," Marshall said impatiently, twirling the hair in his ear.

"That is correct," Authority confirmed.

Bony nodded like a schoolmaster approving a student's scholarship certificate. "Then we may proceed. The microchips you discovered are to be used in the circuitry of a Defense project codenamed *Starlight*. Briefly, it's a system that will allow the United States to continue to probe the Soviets' military command communications and air-defence electronic systems, but without the necessity of using spy planes in clandestine overflights of Soviet territory. First test flight takes place in twenty-one days."

Houston's jaw hung open.

"This is to be done by a radically new satellite development using a breakthrough in advanced surveillance radar. It has enormous power at the flight levels bombers use. The heart of the new system is the invention of the microchips you found in the crash."

I raised my hand. "Would they be the chips tagged MIL-Z-0007? Gold-coloured."

"Correct. Several dozen are used in the new circuitry. The important point is that no more spy-plane overflights will be necessary. *No more Korean Air Lines Flight Seven disasters.*"

We leaned forward in another stiff silence. Marshall's finger poised in mid-air, pointing toward his ear. I think we were all asking ourselves the same question: was this an admission of complicity in the Korean airliner's destruction? Had the United States been using the civilian plane as a decoy to test Soviet electronic defences, despite denials from the White House?

Bony went on. "We know that the Soviets know about Operation *Starlight* and its purpose. That's why I'm able to tell you about it. We also know that they are at least three years behind in developing anything like these particular chips. We don't know how the chips got into the hands of the people killed in the plane crash – assuming they knew what was in the container. What we *do* know is this: the

Soviets have made several desperate attempts to get their hands on those chips. We have informers in the international network –"

"International network, sir?" Marshall asked.

He told us about the network of thieves, many American, who worked in plants making microchips. They sold stolen chips to Soviet agents for huge amounts.

"Workers stuff their shoes with them, secretaries hide them in purses and walk out the plant gates. There are ready buyers with lots of cash – agents working out of the Soviet Consulate in San Francisco who cover Silicon Valley. They're smuggled indirectly to Eastern Bloc countries. Containers, parcels and envelopes of chips flow through Hong Kong, Tokyo, Singapore. Some get aboard the trans-Siberian train waiting in Vladivostok."

"How do you know the Russians haven't already got their hands on these important chips, sir?" Marshall asked. "The ones for *Operation Starlight*."

"We're sure of that," Bony affirmed, without explanation. "The chips you found in the crash wreckage are the first concrete evidence that they were being transferred into the wrong hands. The crash, of course, ended that. There may have been some falling out among thieves. These people are professional crooks. Tough. Some are electronics engineers. They know *what* to steal, what brings the highest prices. They'll stop at nothing – murder, blackmail, torture."

Marshall tugged his ear. "Do you think the chips we found were to be trans-shipped through New York? For a European destination?"

"A possibility."

"Not directly to Moscow. Too obvious," Marshall suggested.

Bony turned to Authority, an action that indicated he had nothing more to say.

Gilbertson's lips twitched. "A year ago we traced a shipment of stolen chips from New York to Zug –"

"Zug?"

"Small town in Switzerland. From there Silicon Valley chips go east to two big customers – Moscow and Peking." He eyed us sharply. "Big bucks are involved. We broke one shipment, a heist in California, involving four million dollars. Fortunately we broke it before they had a chance to ship it out."

Marshall said, "I had no idea –"

"Few do," Gilbertson said, reaching for his attaché case. He opened the lid.

"By the way, this will help speed up your investigation," he said, placing a black binder in front of Marshall.

I leaned over. It was embossed: *Maintenance and Servicing Record, Novajet N23456J.*

FIVE

I stared at Authority, and at Bony, skilled poker players
waiting for the next card to drop. Marshall obliged.

"Where the hell did you find this?" He whipped off his
glasses and held the binder close to re-check the Novajet's
registration number.

The FBI and we were not in confrontation, but there was a
special FBI brand of silence before Authority replied.

"In the drawer of a filing cabinet in a factory in San Jose,
California," he said stiffly.

"I went there," I said. "To see Beech, the vice-president.
To ask for this document."

"Well – there it is. Should make your work easier."

"I'll never say another bad word about the FBI."

"Have you?" The slightest twitch pulsed his lip.

"I was IIC on a Major. Your guys gave me a hard time
when I overlooked the fact that a murder had been
committed aboard the plane before it crash-landed and
killed everybody else." I paused. "Have you identified the
mysterious male corpse found in the Novajet crash, sir?"

Marshall looked up sharply. It had been his question to
ask.

"Not yet," Gilbertson replied. "And we still haven't
found Beech."

"Mrs. Beech told me he's in Tokyo."

"How did you get to see Mrs. Beech?"

"I visited the Beech household."

Authority and Bony exchanged glances. "The house is locked," Authority said. "Nobody answers the front-gate communications set-up."

"They did when I was there."

"When was that?"

"Day before yesterday."

"We couldn't get an answer."

"Maybe they've gone away."

Authority scribbled a note. "What did Mrs. Beech say?"

"That her husband was in Tokyo. On business. Would be several weeks. Vague. Then changed her mind and said it might be three months."

Marshall fiddled with his ear tuft. He looked at Authority.

"Where does this Angelica Oraschuk fit in, sir?"

"Beech's mistress."

"You seem sure."

Authority's eyes hardened. "We are."

I wondered how the FBI could be certain.

"Do you think she knows where Beech is?" Marshall asked.

"Undoubtedly. But we can't find her, either."

I suggested the obvious. "They might both be in Tokyo."

"We've contacted Interpol. The Japanese police are checking Narita's arrivals suspects' data bank."

I made another obvious suggestion – my air accident detective training surfacing: check and re-check and never overlook the obvious. "Mrs. Beech may be lying."

"Of course."

"Beech is vice-president of engineering of the company," Marshall observed. "Do you think *he* selects what microchips to steal?"

"Possibly." Gilbertson chewed his lip.

There was nothing more to discuss. As we stood to leave, thoughts nagged. About two mysterious missing people. I wondered what they looked like: was Beech a handsome tall business executive with an authoritative and commanding appearance? And Angelica Oraschuk? Her first name suggested beauty – with a figure to match. And a voice to move a man's heart.

"Thank you, sir." Marshall clutched the binder under his arm: he didn't seem to want to trust it to his briefcase. "This will speed things up."

"The airplane changed hands like a quarter coin in a video-game arcade," Houston exclaimed.

"Less than a thousand hours flight time since it came out of the factory door," I said.

"But *four* owners," Marshall growled.

"The bloodey autopilot," I added.

The maintenance records showed that when the plane was on autopilot, it tended to fly with a slight nose-up attitude. As a result, fuel consumption went up a bit. Attempts had been made to correct it by adjustments to the autopilot computer. But each successive owner had given up, and none had replaced the computer.

"Owner Number Two, Cloro Banana Corporation, got rid of it less than a month after they bought it," Marshall said, turning the pages. "The third owner, Astro Air Company, hung on to it for only four months. Then *they* sold it." He turned to Liss, the electronics expert. "How much does an autopilot computer of this type cost?"

"Twelve thousand dollars. Knock off three thousand for a second-hand job."

"Don't kid me Cloro Banana couldn't cough up twelve grand," Houston asserted. "They're worth billions. Got a fleet of executive aircraft."

"Perhaps their pilots didn't like the Novajet," I said.

"Because it flew slightly nose-up?" Marshall asked incredulously.

I shook my head. "From my business experience I've learned some pilots are prejudiced against certain aircraft. Don't feel comfortable flying them. The Novajet pilots could have used the autopilot fault as an excuse to ask management to get rid of it. Spun a yarn about potential danger."

"I can't believe that," said Marshall. He turned to Liss.

"Contact Cloro Banana. Ask them why they sold the plane. You'll have to be diplomatic."

"What about the first owner, Starsound Petroleum? And Astro Air?"

"Them too."

Liss whispered into his tape recorder, and left.

Marshall swivelled his chair and stared at the wall. Behind him, on the windowsill, was the sign that had been there since I'd first met him at the Bureau. It announced: *To my crew – please be reasonable and do it my way. The Captain.* It had been presented to him when he'd resigned from airline service fourteen years ago and gone into accident investigation. The resignation had been sudden. He'd been captain of a Boeing 747 from Paris to New York forced to make an emergency landing at Boston's Logan International. A steadily decreasing hydraulic pressure – a mechanic hadn't replaced a five-cent leaky rubber seal – had caused the landing flaps to droop during the last half of the trans-Atlantic flight. On the approach he'd tested the flaps, but they'd refused to stay locked in landing position. Logan ATC instructed him to jettison fuel and make a no-flaps landing. Pilots hated Logan with its long over-the-sea approach to the runway threshold, especially in a crosswind, and it was with a blustery thirty-five-knot crosswind that he headed in. A sudden wind shear – turbulence at ground level – could toss even a 747 off course during the last vital seconds to touchdown: such a wind had slammed a three-engine jet into the seawall at Logan years ago, killing all aboard.

Nobody at NSTB asked Marshall why he resigned. But everybody had heard how he'd pulled off a perfect no-flaps crosswind landing with the 747's huge snout overhanging the concrete at the landward end of the runway by ten feet. At the party they threw when he hung up his cap for the last time, he accepted the framed inscription with a smile, but had never sat on an airborne flight deck again.

He adjusted his glasses and found the engine servicing schedule in the thick binder.

"Left-hand engine had the same flight hours as the airframe," he said. "Nine-hundred and sixty-six. Right-hand had five-hundred and forty-nine hours –"

"It was a rebuilt engine," Houston interrupted.

"Sold as a re-built of course," I said.

He nodded. "Re-built by Pegasus Aero Engines."

"Solid company," I asserted.

They designed and manufactured the engine for the Dragonjet, the latest of a long line of executive aircraft manufactured by Fairwind Aviation Corporation, of California. I was familiar with the aircraft because I flew it as a ferry pilot before I started my charter company. When I lost my family and resigned from NTSB I didn't care where I went or what I did – as long as it took me away from scenes of grisly gore. Ferrying aircraft from Fairwind's factory to customers across the States and around the world helped take my mind off personal problems. I hadn't cared where I went, nor where I rested my head at night – if rest came to blot out the vision of that smoking wreckage – the screams of my trapped kids, and Sarah's.

"Here's something that'll interest you, Doyle," Marshall peered at an entry in the schedule. "Fuel filter of the right-hand engine was replaced twice after the last two-hundred-and-fifty-hour inspection."

"Show me the requirement."

The schedule simply stated, *Replace fuel filter element.* Alongside the column the service engineer had written *Replaced*, with the date. There was another notation: *Element replaced*, with a date two weeks later, and the initials J.M.G. in both places.

"What do the initials stand for?"

"John M. Griffin."

I jotted in my notebook. The Novajet's servicing and maintenance had been entrusted to Eaglewing Aviation Services Incorporated, at San Francisco International. They had a branch at Sea-Tac and I had used their services when my company was young. As business expanded during the better days of air chartering I convinced my bank manager that a loan running into six figures would allow me to expand my fleet, and it would pay us to do our own servicing. I bought three more aircraft: two Piper Senacas and, the pride of our fleet, a Cessna Citation, a sleek twin-jet that I used to park under my office window to admire when it wasn't flying. I cancelled our contract with Eaglewing and we ran our own servicing and maintenance operation.

Houston unwrapped a sandwich and took a generous bite. He turned to Marshall.

"Gonna call Griffin?"

"And deprive Doyle of personally quizzing the only guy who's seen the mysterious Beech?"

"That's an assumption." I grinned.

Houston swallowed. "A safe one. Beech must have given Griffin this service schedule."

I turned to the big flip-over sheets behind Marshall's

desk. He had black-crayoned headings in bold letters:
WHO; DATE; ASSIGNMENT; DUE; COMPLETED:
COMMENTS. Houston's name was under WHO; below
ASSIGNMENT was Oil Sample. DUE showed today's date.
I pointed to it.

"Has the spectrometric analysis come through?"

"Negative. No metallic particles in the oil."

Bradley's name was farther down. He was in charge of the
Structures Group. His assignment: to establish if two
passenger seats had been removed from the Novajet to make
room for the wooden crate. Marshall had scribbled: seats
removed before take-off.

"Have you found Customs forms or address labels yet?"

He looked disappointed. "No. Customs are checking
their records."

"What's the weather like on site?"

"Late snow. Three inches at the beginning of the week."

We discussed other details before the meeting broke up. I
went along to the lab, but couldn't find Turney.

"Off today," his assistant explained. "He's – er, taking
chemotherapy."

"Oh –"

"Anything I can do, Mr. Trimboli?"

"Is the Novajet fuel-test rig ready?"

It wasn't. But he showed me the set-up. It was in the big
lab. As he pointed to this instrument and that bit of
equipment I had to admit that Turney was well-organized,
despite his sloppy appearance. Would I dress neatly and be
well-groomed if I knew that I was going to die in six months
– that was the latest rumour around the labs; that they'd be
looking for a new director in half a year. He'd had a new
Novajet taken from the airplane manufacturer's production
line – the power invested in the NTSB never failed to
astonish me – and parked it by the side of the rig. New

wing-tip tanks had been bolted on, shining like slim, silver fish. A computer terminal display unit was nearby.

I tapped the gleaming wing. "No change to the fuel system?"

"How d'you mean, sir?"

"All you've done is disconnected the new plane's fuel gauges and led wires down to these." I indicated the fuel gauges from the crashed plane.

"That's correct, sir."

"No change to the tanks and the fuel sensors inside them?"

"No sir."

"What's the holdup?" I inquired.

"A couple of test flowmeters." Flowmeters were instruments that showed the rate of fuel flow, essential for my experiment. "They're on their way from the makers."

"When will they be here?"

"Promised for Tuesday. It'll take only a couple of hours to install them."

I was disappointed. But there was nothing I could do about it. I glanced at my watch. There was time to catch United's West Coast evening flight if I hurried. And if I missed it I could grab the jump seat on the flight deck of any other scheduled airline: all air-accident investigators had that right. My ride would be free: NTSB got the bill either way.

John M. Griffin shot me a twitchy look.

"You can't pussyfoot around with safety, Mr. Trimboli." His eyes bulged.

"And so –?"

"I re-examined the filters eighteen flying hours after I replaced them on March first." He stabbed a fingertip on the photostated copy of the relevant pages of the

Maintenance and Servicing Schedule Marshall had given me.

"Why?"

His eyes focused on mine like a pair of hyperthyroid grapes.

"I had a hunch to take it apart."

"Hardly a rational way to service an aircraft." Listen to who's criticizing a guy for acting on hunches. I turned the page. "The requirements are clearly laid out."

"Good thing I did," he went on, ignoring my censure. "The element inside was decomposing –"

"Decomposing?"

"It's made of a special cloth material. It was soft and starting to break up. Could lead to clogged fuel lines."

The pipes Houston and I had inspected had been clear – no sign of clogging. Had this guy caught something before it happened? Had somebody sabotaged a fuel filter, causing fuel starvation?

"You reported it to Inspection, of course?" I looked around the lofty hangar where a dozen executive planes were being serviced. On the far side were glass-fronted offices with signs: Parts Store; Radio and Navigation Servicing; Inspection.

"Of course," he said, looking offended.

"What did Inspection say?"

"Faulty product." His eyes took fire. "They *always* say that." He waved his arms agitatedly, and his hand smacked the shining surface of the Falcon jet we were standing near. "Excuse themselves by blaming the manufacturer." He stepped forward, invading my private territory. I took a backward step to ease my discomfort.

"Would you mind repeating that? I'm not sure I heard right."

He did, and added, "The manufacturer covers his ass by

making goddamned sure his paperwork's in order. But he allows *his* inspection department to pass shoddy products as safe." Aware that he had worked himself up, he stepped back. "You can't pussyfoot around with safety," he repeated.

"Agreed."

"Take that filter. Company that makes it is a major supplier to the aviation industry. Been making fuel and oil filters for forty years. When I learned the trade twenty years ago they turned out a one-hundred-percent product. Never failed. Why? Because they had a strict inspection department before the stuff went out the factory door. Manufactured strictly to government regulations. Then, bit by bit, their standards dropped. Poorly-formed rivet here, a lousy weld there." He waved his arms again. "Now they turn out real shitty filters. That's why I re-inspected the Ling plane when it came back from Mexico."

"Mexico?" I tucked that into my memory cells.

"The flight put eighteen hours on the aircraft."

"When was that?"

"End of January. It's in the schedule."

"Let's go back to what you said. If the filter maker's inspection standards have dropped, how come the FAA hasn't cancelled the company's manufacturing licence?" A manufacturer of aircraft components had to turn out perfect products to meet the Federal Aviation Administration's specifications."

"Not going to step into that puddle," he snapped.

"You're a man of firm convictions and strong opinions. You may need to justify them at an inquiry."

He stiffened. "Inquiry?"

"It's unusual for a public inquiry to be held in a case like this – investigation of the crash of a private plane – but the Bureau has the power to recommend that a public inquiry be held."

He stared at me with those bulging eyes, looking a bit unsure of himself. Then, with discernible resolve, he pushed doubt away.

"I'll repeat that in a court of law. The policy is all wrong." He pointed to a single-engine light plane in a corner of the hangar. "That plane's electrical generator crapped out after only three hours flight time. Original equipment cost three hundred bucks. Bought from a so-called reputable manufacturer. They took it out and replaced it with an automobile alternator, costing sixty-five bucks. Perfectly legal, according to the authorities. Been in that plane for more'n seven hundred hours and still works good as new."

"Be more specific." I knew what he was driving at: the argument had come up at the Bureau. Maybe he had a new point.

"How come an alternator for a car is made to the same level of quality acceptance as one made to airworthiness standards?"

"The argument is usually put the other way around. How come a part made to strict aircraft specifications can be satisfactorily replaced by an automobile part?"

"The law says you can install the car alternator if the box it comes in is sealed and unopened," he went on, slapping the Falcon Jet. "You can't pull off the road if your engine quits at twenty thousand feet." He stared into my face with those spherical eyes, then leaned close and said in a confidential tone, "I'm keeping a written record of things I hear about."

He shut up. I was afraid to say anything in case he should withdraw his confidence.

"Every time I hear of somebody substituting a commercial component like an automobile part for an aircraft part it goes into the book."

"Did you find any such substitution on the Novajet that

crashed? Fuel Filter, for example."

"No."

"You seem sure."

He locked eyes with me again. "I know every component and part of that Novajet's engines. *Everything*."

"Then how come you suddenly had a hunch and opened up the fuel filter when the plane returned from Mexico?"

"Pure hunch. She was like my own baby crying for me. Been servicing her since she started coming to Eaglewing."

I turned the pages of the engine servicing schedule. Griffin's initials appeared on all entries.

"I wouldn't let her out of this hangar unless she was operating perfectly. My boss never had any trouble signing her off."

I looked at the Inspector-in-Charge's signature written against each inspection period. *John G. Fess.*

He smoothed away a tuck in the sleeve of his ultra-white coveralls. I looked down at his gleaming shoes, and then up at the neatly trimmed haircut and the precisely-trimmed moustache. I'd heard about men such as Griffin: they were known in the industry as Triple A types, perfectionists who made aircraft servicing and maintenance as carefully honed an art as the composing of a piece of classical music. Perfectionism became an obsession. Not surprising that he abhorred the use of commercial parts as substitutes for aircraft components in non-critical applications.

"You must meet Mr. Beech often," I said.

"Not often," he said in a cautious voice, looking evasive. He added quickly, "Usually he sends his secretary with the schedule when the plane comes in for servicing."

I was tempted to ask what she looked like. Instead: "Most aircraft owners let the servicing company keep the schedule."

He hefted a shoulder in a none-of-my-business gesture.

"What's Mr. Beech like?" I asked suddenly.

Again, an evasive glance. "Good guy," he said with pretended conviction.

"Isn't *he* an engineer?"

"Vice-president of the engineering department of Ling."

"Must be a big outfit to own an executive jet."

"Guess so," he replied uninterestedly.

"But you've only met him occasionally."

He circled his eyes. "Two or three times. As I said, his secretary comes with the schedule."

"What does she say to you?"

"Too stuck up to speak. Just hands me the schedule."

"What does Ling make?" I asked offhandedly.

"Plastic toys and games. Maybe video games – not sure."

"Plastic toys?"

He led me to a workbench and unlocked a gleaming red toolbox. He took out several plastic toy vehicles: red fire engine; white ambulance; a yellow sports car like the one Houston had vroomed across the table.

"I've been meaning to take them home for my kids. But they've already got dozens."

"Presents from Mr. Beech?"

He nodded. "Gave them to everybody here." He gestured toward technicians working on other aircraft. "Probably rejects off the production line."

Beech the Santa Claus? Or doing *himself* a good PR job? Or PR-ing his company? I pointed to the inside of the yellow sports car. "What do you suppose these moulded brackets are for?"

He peeked inside. "Maybe they fit electric motors here."

"With electronic controls, eh?"

"Maybe."

"Microchip controls?" I persisted.

He shrugged.

"You're an *engine* technician," I said. "But did you know about the autopilot on the crashed plane?"

"Autopilot?" His voice was suspicious.

"Autopilot."

"It had a fault," he said with quicksilver reversal from suspicion to frankness. "Caused the aircraft to fly slightly nose-up. Heard about it from Avionics Department."

"Who's in charge there?"

"Elliot Provost."

"Please take me to him – er, just a moment. Figure somebody sabotaged that fuel filter?"

"Sabotaged?"

"Sabotaged," I repeated.

"Never gave it a thought." His eyes gyrated. "Whoever would want to do that?"

"I don't know. Filters don't suddenly disintegrate after eighteen hours of flight time."

"I didn't say it disintegrated," he said defensively. "I said it was starting to break up."

"You also said it was decomposing. Explain precisely what you mean."

"Have you examined the filters from the crashed aircraft?"

"Yes."

"And they were in good condition?" he asked.

"Yes." To forestall another question I added, "Explain what *you* mean."

"The element, the plasticized cloth cylinder that fits inside the casing, had started to break up. Little bits of plastic material had loosened."

"How big's a little bit?" I demanded.

"At the edges," he replied, a defensive note in his voice.

"How big?" I insisted.

"One thou of an inch."

"One thousandth of an inch?" I exclaimed. "That's smaller than some of the junk in jet fuel the filter's supposed to catch."

"Nevertheless, it *was* breaking up."

"How many of these bits did you discover?"

"Two."

"And you suggest that could lead to clogged fuel pipes?"

"Eventually. If more bits broke off."

A perfectionist of perfectionists. I looked into the open drawer of his toolbox. Rows of wrenches and screwdrivers were laid out in velvet-lined recesses in ascending order of size. On a shelf above the toolbox were capped glass jars containing bolts, nuts and washers, the contents of each jar identified with precisely hand-lettered labels. The workbench had been scrupulously scrubbed until the wood was white.

"I think we can rule out sabotage on that score," I said. "Will you please take me to Mr. Provost?"

I explained the accident to Provost. "You know about the minor problem with the autopilot?"

"When Ling took delivery of the aircraft Captain Phillips reported the autopilot fault on the snag sheet," he said.

"You saw the sheet?"

"Of course. We ran a test on the computer. Couldn't find anything wrong. We checked the flight controls. A-okay all the way through. I've got the records here."

He got up from his desk and searched a filing cabinet.

"Novajet N23456J. Ling International Import-Export Corporation." He read from a file flap, and withdrew the file.

"We removed the computer for a bench test." A slight

smile lit his face. "Electronics still the weakest link in aviation."

I thought of the fuel gauges. "Maybe."

"Couldn't find anything wrong with it. Checked out perfectly. We re-installed it, got Beech's permission to test-fly the aircraft and – you guessed it – the aircraft, when on autopilot, tended to fly nose-up."

"And then?"

"I made a report to our client, Mr. Beech. I recommended replacing the computer – it would cost eleven and a half thousand plus labour – thirteen thousand in all, but he turned it down. Can't understand some clients." He shook his head. "Invest more than one and a half million in a plane, hire two pilots on twenty-four-hour call, engage us to service and maintain the aircraft, but won't invest thirteen thousand dollars in what we call 'remedial servicing' – repairing a fault before it has a chance to develop into something dangerous."

"Do you think the faulty autopilot could have caused the aircraft to crash?"

"You said it was fuel starvation."

"That's the evidence so far."

"Simultaneous flameouts on both engines would point to that." He thought a moment. "Can't see a connection between the autopilot and the crash. You can always switch off the autopilot if it acts up badly."

"Have you met this guy Beech?"

"No. But I've spoken to him on the phone."

"What sort of man do you think he is?"

Provost opened his hands palm up on his desk. "Well, Mr. Trimboli, I just told you he refused to shell out thirteen thousand dollars on a million-and-a-half investment."

"Mean guy?"

"I didn't say that."

"Sorry –" A guy who insisted on Novajet replacements parts – no less-expensive commercial junk – couldn't be mean.

We discussed the fuel system, but Provost was an electronics expert and knew only basics about fuel systems: modern planes were so complex it was all that a man or woman could do to keep current with the state of the art in a single field.

"How come Mr. Beech took away the maintenance and servicing schedule after the plane was serviced?" I asked as we prepared to part.

Provost again opened his hands. "I don't know. Most clients are happy to leave them here. Nobody likes paperwork."

"And you never saw him?" I reiterated.

"No."

I asked him to introduce me to Fess, Inspector-in-Charge, responsible for ultimately signing aircraft off as safe-to-fly after they'd been serviced. Fess impressed me: he emanated the type of strict self-discipline and the ability to impart it to others that were possessed by university professors of the old school. He also assured me that Griffin was "the most thorough aero-engine service technician."

I thanked him. He arranged for a company station wagon to take me to *Holy Ghost*. I'd parked it on the far side of the General Aviation lot, about a mile away. It was a long trip around, past several airline terminals. In the distance I caught a glimpse of San Francisco Bay, metally blue under the evening sun. The sea was kicking up again.

"Drop me off at Visitors' Reception," I told the driver.

"I'm the owner of the Cessna 172," I said to the young woman behind the counter, and gave the aircraft's registration number. "I said I'd be here just for the day. Something's come up. I want to change that to all-night parking."

She looked at a plan on the wall. A host of coloured pins

indicated parked airplanes. "That's fine, sir." She altered the records.

I went to the lounge and buried my nose in a highball. I wouldn't be flying again until tomorrow morning: ample time to encompass the eight-hours-from-bottle-to-throttle rule.

At nine-thirty I went to the restaurant and eased my way through an enormous lobster with accessories. I ordered a peach Melba for dessert and allowed it to slide down with the help of a couple of Drambuies. I didn't stick the NTSB with the bill: I used Trimboli's Air Charterers' credit card. With time to kill, I returned to the near-empty lounge, picked out the most comfortable-looking armchair, spread a copy of the *San Francisco Chronicle* over my face, and fell into a half-sleep despite my rumbling stomach.

An hour later I awoke, and walked under a moonless sky between rows of parked planes to *Holy Ghost*. Unlocking the cabin door, I climbed into the back seat and opened a suitcase. I took out a pair of jeans, dark sweater and soft running shoes. I removed my business suit and put on the outfit, feeling lighter and ready for action. I picked up a battered lunchpail – a borrowing from one of Pender's technicians – casually strolled back to the General Aviation centre, and rented a car. In a half-hour I was clear of the airport traffic and heading south on Highway 101 with the speedometer needle five mph below the limit: this wasn't the time to be flagged down by a trooper.

A traffic accident near Redwood City snarled me for twenty minutes, but I didn't mind: as more of the world went to sleep the better it suited me. South of Redwood City I dawdled, had a forty-five-minute coffee break at a roadside cafe, and continued south. It was after midnight when I eased past the San Jose plant and parked in a side street. I sat for fifteen minutes in silence, grabbed the lunchpail, and pressed the door handle. The door opened with a metallic grunt, and I stepped on to the sidewalk.

Few cars went by on the main road. Diagonally opposite was a sign, Ling International Import-Export Corp., Inc. Farther along, a truck backed into the receiving bay of another factory. A security van drove past. Under the glare of the street lights I saw the driver animatedly chatting to the man at his side. I had an urge to laugh: they didn't even look at me, a man in dark clothes clutching a lunch pail going to work after midnight when most plants in San Jose didn't work nightshifts. I waited for it to disappear, and crossed the road.

Easy. A rear window slid under the persuasion of a fine-pointed tool. No bars, no wire mesh and, surprisingly, no burglar alarm. I had prepared for that, with an electronic smothering device that traced the sensing device and put it out of action instantly. But it didn't always work. I waited outside for ten minutes, crouching against the wall. The rumble of a distant train slid along on the chilly air, and the swish of cars on a nearby freeway zipped and zapped. Then I went in over the windowsill, swearing when I ripped a rubber glove on an obstacle. I left the window open: experience had taught me the value of an instant escape route.

My flashlight picked out wooden crates stacked against a wall in a big room. There was a bench. The only things on the bench were a claw hammer and a pair of pliers. I tiptoed to a door and encircled the handle with the palm of my glove, expecting an alarm, braced to switch on the device – or dash to the window. Tightening my grip, I turned. Pulled the door open. An office with an executive-type desk and chair, carpet on the floor, and two filing cabinets. There was another door opposite. I opened it and peered through. A desk with a typewriter. The blonde woman's desk: front entrance hall.

An empty plant with no manufacturing facilities.

Didn't make sense.

I crept back to the big room and examined a crate near the end of the stack. It was empty. I counted: forty-seven crates. Then I set about pulling each crate from the wall to see if there was a door concealed behind the stack. No door. And each crate was empty. I looked for address labels – labels of any kind that would identify the contents. No labels; rusty metal staples where labels had been attached. No words or identifying marks on the wood.

Puzzled, I moved back to the office and shone the flashlight on the desk. Beech's or Nordsen's? The framed photograph near the in-tray answered: the boy I'd met at Beech's house. No picture of the boy's mother. Not so strange. The top drawer was unlocked. It held ballpoints, a ruler, paperclips, and rubber bands in the shallow front tray. There were several letters. I shuffled them in the flashlight's glare. Correspondence typed on letterhead of Ling International Import-Export Corporation, Inc. Letters to companies in New York, Chicago, Miami and other cities. Letters with typing errors that had been corrected by the old-fashioned correction-fluid method. The dates held the answer: they were two years old.

Other drawers contained file folders with letters of inquiry about quotations for kid's games and puzzles, all with ancient dates. Some were so old the paper was browning at the edges.

Two letters in the in-tray. One addressed to a firm in Los Angeles stating that the delivery of the fifty dozen sets of Magic Magnet Game No. D-146 had unfortunately been delayed because of a labour dispute in Taiwan. The other was addressed to a Tokyo company confirming Ling

International's order for six gross of Constellation Computer Puzzle Fun Game, with an underlined instruction that the order be air-freighted *immediately*.

I glanced at the initials at the bottom of the letters: WOB/AS. Dictated by Wilbur O. Beech; typed by Angelica Oraschuk.

The nearby filing cabinet was unlocked. It contained files of correspondence. I read several letters. Similar in content to those on Beech's desk. The second filing cabinet was locked. I worked the tumblers with a fine steel probe. After a bit of fussing they went my way and I pulled open the top drawer. Empty. So were the others. I swept my fingers around. Inspected the tips for dust that would indicate the drawers had contained letters. Nothing. But at the back of the top drawer my rubber-sheathed fingertips dredged up a little metal clip of the type that flattens the metal tangs of loose-leaf binders such as those used for aircraft Maintenance and Servicing Records. The FBI wasn't perfect.

I stood with legs crossed, leaning against the open filing cabinet. No manufacturing facilities; no plastic toys; and nothing connected with microchips. Letters of inquiry about kids' games and puzzles. Outdated letters.

The air stirred near me. A scuffling movement behind. A searing pain at the back of my head. Eyeballs blazed with constellations of blue flashes, the drawer edge rose and slammed my chin – and everything went black.

SIX

A butcher's cleaver was hacking a furrow through my brain. I opened my eyes. There was a dim light. A shadow moved.

"Relax – Mr. Trimboli. Keep your head still."

I stopped rolling my head from side to side. But the booming echoed – bang, bang, BANG.

"You lost – a lot of blood."

That explains the banging: no blood in the brain. Operating on dry cells. I was aware of a throbbing in my jaw. My back seared with pain. My left arm – my good arm – jerked spasmodically.

"Don't fight it."

The shadow became a shape. It receded and returned. A vague form became concrete: a young woman with a freckled face. Pretty. Red hair. Ridiculous cap. Nurse's cap.

"Please keep still. You're connected to a transfusion –"

Consciousness was slipping away. With a huge effort I struggled to keep from going under. My mouth felt dry.

"Transfusion?" I heard a voice croak. My jaw wouldn't open fully.

"You were stabbed in the back. Three times."

"Would – would you mind repeating – er, that. I'm not sure – I heard right."

"You were stabbed three times in the back. Lost blood."

I rolled my eyes upward. A plastic bag hung from a

fixture. Plastic pipes led down. Like a fuel system.

Another face appeared. Man's face. Fingers touched muscles around my eyes. Caring fingers. A beam of light pierced my eyeball. I squinted and shrank back into the pillow.

"Sorry – let's try it again." He had a kind face with no-nonsense written all over it.

I forced my eyes to stay open while he shone the light.

"Try to rest. I'll be back this afternoon."

"Where am I?"

"In the general hospital."

"Which – general – hospital?" There was something tied around my jaw that inhibited it working.

"San Francisco –"

"But where's *Holy Ghost?*"

"Do you wish to speak to the chaplain?"

"*Holy Ghost* –"

"How many fingers do you see?" He waved a finger under my nose.

"One – but somebody's got to fly *Holy Ghost* back to Seattle. It's collecting parking fees."

The lines around the no-nonsense mouth softened.

"We seem to be talking about different things. You've had a concussion. Who or what is *Holy Ghost?*"

"An airplane I own. Parked at the airport. Overduly parked."

He grinned. "*Holy Ghost* needs resurrection?"

I explained. God – the pain in my head. I tried to think of my office number. It took a long time to form into numerals in my brain. I gave Pender's name. "I'll have someone take care of it, Mr. Trimboli."

"How long will I be here, doctor?"

He shook his head. "You've had a bad time. Somebody hit you on the head with a hammer. **The x-rays show it.**

Then there're stab wounds, jaw trauma, wrenched arm –"

"What happened to my arm?" I demanded, alarmed.

"You must have fallen on it when you were hit on the head. It's not broken – twisted."

"So – how long?"

"Can't say. Few more days at least."

"Few more days? How long have I been here?"

"Two days."

"Two? How did I get here?"

"Police said a couple of teenagers found you in a ditch in a lover's lane off Highway 101 south of Redwood City. The cops are very interested in why you wore rubber gloves."

"In a ditch? I remember standing by the filing –" I shut up. "And have I been unconscious for two days?"

He nodded. "Now try to get some rest. I'll have the nurse wake you every hour to make sure you haven't lapsed into unconsciousness." He smiled before moving away. Then he turned back. "By the way, the police asked me when you might be able to make a statement."

"Oh –"

"I told them to come back in a few days."

He moved out of range.

I closed my eyes and fell asleep. A moment later someone gently tapped my shoulder.

"Mr. Trimboli." A pretty face and a pert cap hovered over me.

"I'm sorry, Dr. Whitson's orders. Have to wake you every hour."

"But I just fell asleep."

"That was an hour ago – we have to wake you to make sure –"

"I'm not in the hands of the Holy Ghost," I murmured, slipping back into oblivion.

* * *

The policeman came three days later. I was sitting up in bed. My back felt better, but the dressings itched. They had removed the bandage from my jaw and replaced it with a simple stick-on plaster. It wobbled when I spoke.

"And you woke up here?" the cop re-affirmed.

"Yes."

He looked down at his notebook. Outside the lounge window, patients and visitors strolled over the lawns.

"Is there anything you'd like to add, Mr. Trimboli?"

He had droopy eyelids over slit eyes that gave the impression he was used to being told lies. I had said I'd been in a bar – "I forget the name of the place – in downtown San Francisco and these two guys –"

He'd written it all down in schoolboy's even handwriting, the look on his face proclaiming he didn't believe a word.

"I wish to add that I want to make a statement to the FBI." His eyelids shot up. "Nothing personal," I added.

"Muggings are handled by the local police."

"But the reason I was mugged is a matter for the FBI."

"You'd better explain," he said, with the resignation of a lifetime of experience.

I sketched the background, but didn't tell him I had burglarized the Ling plant. Then we went back to the ward and I showed him my NTSB identification card.

"I guess it's okay," he said doubtfully. "Interstate transportation *is* a matter for the FBI. And if you've already been in touch with the Bureau – well." He put away his notebook. "Who's your contact at FBI headquarters?"

I told him. He asked the nurse if he could use the phone. He asked for Gilbertson, and spoke quietly, casting a look from time to time in my direction from beneath pendant eyelids. His face gave nothing away. He put down the phone.

"Very well." His face showed the first glimmer of feeling

since he'd come: he looked relieved. "You'll be contacted by a local agent of the Bureau."

He left. Five minutes later the phone rang. It was Marshall. He asked how I was.

"Better than a couple of days ago. I'm gonna persuade the doctor to discharge me when I see him tomorrow." I fingered the light bandage around my back that replaced the heavy swathing. "What's happening at your end?"

"The rig is ready for your test."

"I'll call you tomorrow. I think I'll be okay. My head's already airworthy."

"There's some good news. Downey discovered a label. In the jacket pocket of the unidentified cadaver. Typewritten address. Blood messed up the wording, but the labs gave it the infra-red treatment." He paused. "Are you standing up or lying down?"

"Standing up."

"Better sit."

I sat on the edge of the bed. "I'm sitting."

He cleared his throat, "The label's addressed to W.O. Beech, c/o Cafe Orientale, 649A Kaiserstrasse, Frankfurt, West Germany."

It didn't sink in.

"Would you mind repeating –"

He growled a repetition.

"But why was the label in the guy's pocket?"

"Theory around here is that it was their intention to attach labels *after* they got to New York, before trans-shipping to a regular carrier."

"What does Gilbertson say? You told him, of course."

"Yes – he said nothing."

That fitted. Authority wasn't the type to dish out opinions, or information.

"This Beech guy's either a code name or a real guy who

gets around a lot. Did you check Customs for records of declaration forms?"

"They reported back earlier today. No record of any shipment from a company named Ling. Or to the Cafe Orientale."

After another inquiry about my health, Marshall put down the phone. I replaced the receiver, but it rang again. A man called Durell, FBI, San Francisco. He came in half an hour. I told him everything. He taped it.

"I'll put it on the secure line to Washington, Mr. Trimboli. Good day."

And then I felt foolish. What had I accomplished by my burglary? Gilbertson had already done it, and got the Maintenance and Servicing Record. I had found nothing, discovered nothing new: Gilbertson must have seen the old letters. Then my brain cells conjoined in a flash of excitement. I *had* accomplished a hell of a lot: I had *proved* something that we had up to now only assumed. Whoever had attacked me *knew* that the operations of Ling International Import-Export Corporation were illegal, and was prepared to kill me to prevent that secret being revealed. But I'd paid dearly for it. Lucky to be alive. They'd probably left me for dead. As I slipped under the covers I started making a mental list of suspects.

I sat before the test bench and checked the gauges. They showed zero. I glanced up at the factory-new Novajet before us.

"Fill up," I said to Turney. "To the top of the tanks."

They'd brought a refuelling truck up to the outside wall. A fuel hose zig-zagged across the floor. As they filled the tanks, the fuel gauge numerals whirled. They were the gauges from the crashed Novajet. When the gauges showed full I said, "Please check with the dipsticks that the tanks are full."

They opened the inspection holes and poked in the wooden dipsticks. They were wet right up to the tops of the tanks.

Then came the routine bit. I switched on the pumps immersed in the tanks, went through the drill of working the valves so that our simulated flight took off on the internal wing tanks, switching to wing-tip tanks until they were empty, and then switching back to the internal wing tanks. We couldn't run the plane's engines indoors, of course, and the fuel pumps were hooked up to an electric supply in the lab. The pumped-through fuel was piped back into the refuelling truck outside.

It went well: too well – we ended up in simulated fashion at John F. Kennedy International, New York. And the gauges showed enough fuel left to take us to Newark or Boston, the alternative emergency airports in case of foul weather in New York.

Marshall scowled. "That proves the crashed gauges are all right. Now where the hell do we go?"

"I'll tell you where," I said motioning to Turney. "Please check with the dipsticks again."

They stuck them in the internal wing tanks. The sticks were wet for about five inches.

"Now the wing-tip tanks, please."

They inserted the sticks.

"Dry as a bone," the chief technician called down.

"Same here," the man on the opposite wing said.

Marshall got up, looking disappointed. "Everything checks out A-okay for a normal flight. The wing-tip tanks are empty because all their fuel was used up in accordance with the normal procedure before switching to the internal wing tanks, where there's plenty left after flying to New York. We haven't proved *anything*." He glanced at his watch. "I've got a Board meeting –"

"Not so fast," Houston said. "At the crash site there was a bit of spillage where the wing tanks were thrown into the trees."

"Spillage on the trees or on the ground?" I asked.

"Trees, but some dripped on the ground. I was going to dig it out later, but didn't get around to it."

"It's not too late."

"It didn't look significant. But I agree, we should dig it out."

Marshall jotted in his notebook. "I'll get somebody on to it right away," he said, and trudged off.

"Just a second," I called after him. "Please show me the label with the Frankfurt address you found in the clothing of the unidentified male corpse."

Kaiserstrasse was a grubby but wide thoroughfare near the Hauptbahnhof, as districts next to the railway terminals of many cities are. Smells of pickled meats, freshly-baked bread and garbage met me head on. I passed a beer-hall where oompa-oompa-oompa-pa boomed through the open door. Drivers of streetcars angrily clanged bells as jaywalkers crossed the tracks ahead. The beerhall was number fifty-seven. I walked on, passed a row of sex shops where the prurient, the curious, and potential customers gazed with sad faces at the window displays, and waited for the lights to change.

I continued. After three or four blocks Kaiserstrasse's nature changed. The shops became more stylish: little boutiques with silk scarves, fashionable hats, and kid gloves in the windows. The restaurants, too, were classier, and there were sidewalk trees with the delicate leaves of spring unfolding. The numbers over the doors showed five hundred and something. The people were different too. Working people had been at the Hauptbahnhof end; here elegantly-dressed matrons walked equally-groomed poodles, expensively-suited gentlemen with black Homburgs bustled by, and chauffeur-driven Mercedes-Benzes drew up at smart hair-styling salons to let down slim young women with already, it seemed to me, well-coiffured hair.

Number 641-643 – it must be the building on the next corner. I hurried up. Number 649 was a hat shop. Number 649A?

I stared at the floor above, expecting 649A to be a cafe over the hat shop. But there were houseplants on the inside sills and heavy drapes drawn completely across the windows.

I went into the hat shop. A girl behind the counter smiled.

"Excuse me – er, bitte. I'm looking for the Cafe Orientale."

"Upstairs. The entrance is around the corner," she replied in perfect English, and pointed.

"Ah – danke." Drawn drapes in windows of a cafe?

I turned the corner. *Cafe Orientale* was in cursive, gold script on the door. It was locked. There was a sign in German and English: Open seven days a week 8:00 p.m. – 3:00 a.m.

I peered through the glass panel. A faint light showed in a dark corridor leading to stairs. It was six o'clock. I went back to the Parkhotel on Wiesenhüttenplatz and nursed a Scotch in the bar for two hours. Since I'd been on my own I couldn't stand the loneliness of hotel rooms, and hardly that of my apartment. I even shared an office with Pender. Then I had a bath and dressed, and took a taxi to the cafe. I swung open the door. The hall was now brightly lit. Upstairs was a small restaurant, also well lit. Two men were sitting alone at separate tables. A group of young women sat around a table near the back, listening to the loud voice of a solid-looking man with slicked-back hair. A waiter – there appeared to be only one – approached.

"Good evening, sir." My American clothes gave me away. "Would you like to sit here?" He indicated a seat midway between the men's tables and the one where the others sat.

"Fine with me."

He handed me a menu, and withdrew behind a glass counter in which the widest variety of pastries and torten were displayed on white doilies. I looked around, surprised that there was no oriental décor. The menu was jammed with a confusion of grilled sausages, schnitzels, bratwurst, lebkuchen, liver dumpling soup, sauerkraut, and other heavy fare.

When I looked up again the waiter snapped to attention and hurried over. I ordered a veal steak, mashed spuds, and salad.

"And a bottle of Pfalz," I added, recalling the white wine of the region.

I looked at the men. The nearer was sharp-nosed. In his middle sixties. He wore a neatly-pressed dark suit, over-carefully knotted tie as if he'd had several tries doing it, and recently polished worn-heeled shoes. He ate with his elbows close to his sides as if he was nervous. Worker's fingers. Visitor to Frankfurt from small-town Germany, probably the Ruhr. The other man was thirtyish, well-dressed in a relaxed way, and totally unselfconscious. He emanated the cockiness of a man of handsome aspect and means who knew he could approach any woman at a public dancehall and bed her the same night. I didn't like him.

Nor did I like the man he was looking at, the man with shiny hair at the back table. He held the attention of five young women. He spoke perfect English.

"... so I told this man in Stockholm, 'I'm not in the mood tonight, thank you very much. My ex-wife wouldn't like it either'." A couple of girls laughed. "You know me. I'm a cosmopolitan ..."

I sipped wine and took another forkful of veal. Cooked to perfection. The potatoes tasted better than stateside spuds. I'd discovered that European vegetables taste more natural than ours: English lettuce and cucumber; Normandy carrots and peas that titillated the tastebuds; onions from Brittany –

"– when I got to Copenhagen I was in the Valencia." The girls giggled. "And met a sea captain's widow. About forty, and very good looking. Well built too."

Mr. Slicked-back-hair raised a glass to his lips. I studied the women and realized how the restaurant got its name: with one exception they were Chinese and Japanese.

"... well, girls," the voice said, "I'm on my way."

A petite Chinese girl tugged his arm.

"Stay and dance with me," she pleaded.

"Can't tonight. You know me. Like to drop in for a chat. Like to be friendly to all."

He dispensed smiles to everybody, and got up. I glanced at his shoes. Patent leather, pointed like the twin prows of a catamaran sailboat.

"Bye-bye," he said. "Oh – nearly forgot." He picked up a folded newspaper that showed racing result tables. "Enjoy your drinks."

"Thank you for buying them," the girls chorused.

My young dining companion looked them over with an impudent stare. He stuck his fork into a greasy sausage and shoved it into his mouth with a quick movement, chewed vigorously until juice ran from the corner of his mouth and dribbled down his chin. He wiped it away with the back of his hand, eyes on the women.

Soft music sounded from a room at the back of the restaurant. Other patrons appeared, singly, mostly men. A couple of attractive women, who seemed to know each other, said "Guten Abend" to the waiter, and vanished in the direction of the music.

I put down my fork. The waiter approached.

"We have a wide selection of desserts, sir." He presented the menu.

"Any recommendations?"

"Would you like something sweet, sir?"

I glanced at the list of pastries and considered. "I'll stick to the strudel. Will you warm it up? And black coffee, please."

"Thank you, sir."

I glanced at the older man. He was still eating, occasionally stopping to dislodge, with a toothpick, a bit of food from some stubbornly resisting dental obstruction. A row of used picks made a neat pattern around the rim of his plate.

The occidental woman at the table, whose back was towards me, turned and looked across. She smiled. I returned acknowledgement sans encouragement. The waiter came between us. He presented a plate with strudel.

"It's very hot sir. Be careful."

Delicious. Filmy. Melted on the tongue. I was manoeuvring another portion with my fork when a figure appeared at my table.

"Good evening," she said with a slight accent, making no attempt to sit.

"Good evening."

She wore a tastefully designed blue dress. The decolletage was not overdone; only a hint of cleavage showed.

"Have you been to Frankfurt before?"

"A few times." I'd been once.

"I was in America. New York."

"Did you like it?" I sipped coffee.

"Very much." She had eyes that matched the colour of

her dress, fair medium-length hair, natural-colour nail varnish and gave the impression of being a lady. "I was there three months."

"Did you go out of town?"

"Oh, yes." She seemed surprised. "A month in Miami Beach."

"Are you the hostess?" I asked.

"The manager refers to me as that." She smiled, and indicated by a subtle shift of her body that she would like to join me. I ignored it.

"What's his name?"

"Herr – Mr. Heimer."

"I used to know a Mr. Heider."

A slight rounding of the eyes. The pupils dilated the tiniest. Imagination?

"Sounds Scandinavian – not German," she said.

I raised the cup.

"Are you interested in meeting one of our oriental ladies?" she asked.

"The dainty Chinese lady with the long hair is very attractive."

"Would you like to meet her?"

"When I've finished my coffee." The guidelines had been adhered to, the messages exchanged. It was all right to ask, "Will you join me?"

"Thank you."

I motioned to the waiter.

"We've got a new dance band tonight," she said. "I think you'll enjoy it."

"Does Mr. Heimer treat you well?"

She stiffened. Suspicion hardened her eyes.

"Yes – of course. He's a good man. Very kind."

I looked around. The older man had finished dinner and was upending a beer stein. He smothered a burp and called the waiter for another beer. The younger man smacked his lips, got up and walked to the women's table. He spoke to a Japanese girl. She smiled, and rose. He slipped his arm around her waist and guided her toward the back room.

I drained my coffee cup.

"Shall I introduce you now?"

"It doesn't seem necessary."

"Oh, him – he's a regular."

"Okay."

Blue Dress introduced the Chinese woman as Odette.

"Like the girl in Swan Lake," the Chinese girl said, reaching for my left hand. "I think my mother wanted me to be a ballet star."

We walked to the edge of the dance floor.

"My right arm. I can't put it around you."

She passed her arm around it and held me, dancing close, rubbing her pliant body against mine in a sinuous motion. The top of her head came to my chin. There were only three couples on the floor, and we could talk without being overhead.

"Is Herr Heimer a kind man?" I asked abruptly.

Her body sprang away with the reaction of a hand touching a hot kettle. She looked up, eyes wide. Fear lay beneath their black intensity.

"That's a – funny question." Her voice, previously coy and filled with artificial sweetness, had acquired a coarse edge.

"I wondered if he treats you well."

I forced her hand back and we continued dancing. Her body kept four inches distant.

"As well as –" She glanced over her shoulder.

"As well as?" I encouraged.

"As well as any boss in a place like this."

I wondered how many places "like this" she had worked in.

"I hope he doesn't mistreat you."

She pulled her arm around me and pressed her body so close her thighs rubbed against mine with every movement of her legs. How her boss treated her was none of my business: it wasn't her job to talk about her boss.

I was plunged into doubt. The dance floor, the restaurant, a man called Heimer – was that his real name? – the whole ambience of the place seemed unrealistically disconnected with bits of metallic debris littering a forest clearing half a world away. But: the copy of a label found at the site, in my billfold; a label with this address on it. And Beech's name.

The music stopped. She took my hand and led me to a table at the edge of the floor. Other couples had entered. The out-of-towner in the restaurant had finished his beer and was now in the care of a Japanese woman.

"Do you like Frankfurt, Collin?" she asked. It was the name I'd given.

"Bit too busy for me."

She squeezed my hand. "Are you staying long?"

Usual question. The next would be: "What's the name of your hotel?" But she didn't ask it. She tilted her head and examined my features.

"You have an honest face." She paused while her eyes circled my features again. "And you're very good looking."

"There's not much light."

She laughed.

"You're a beautiful young woman. Were you born in China?"

"Thank you. I come from Peking."

"Have you been in the United States?"

"No – I'd love to."

The band started up.

"Shall we?"

My nosiness seemed to have been forgotten, if not

forgiven. She squeezed against me so tightly we moved around the floor like one body. She nestled her cheek against my throat and hummed with minor-key sadness. A tiny hand clutched the back of my neck as my right arm drooped free. Then she suddenly looked up, eyes filled with tears. I steered her to the edge of the floor.

"A drink?"

She shook her head. "It's watered for the girls."

"Coffee?"

"Yes."

We went into the now-crowded restaurant. She excused herself. I ordered coffee. When she returned her face was like new.

"I'm sorry, Collin."

"Are you in trouble?"

She stared at her cup.

"Anything I can do?"

Her eyelids fluttered. Was I a sucker for a trick? She looked at me for several moments.

"You have an honest face. But do you have a truthful heart?"

It sounded like a Chinese proverb. A man may have an honest face, but an untruthful heart. I'd met several in my business.

"I tell the truth." Except when it suited the purpose of an investigation.

"I was fired today. This is my last week here."

I touched her hand. "I'm sorry. Heimer?"

"Yes."

"Did he say why?"

She shook her head. "What'll I do? I've got a little boy to support." Her eyes misted over.

It was too pat, too set up. On the other hand, she *hadn't* asked the name of my hotel, nor pursued the question of the length of my stay. In fact, she'd been curiously incurious about me. I had asked the questions.

"Can't you get a job in another place like this?"

She shook her head. "I hate the work. I want to get out. For my little boy's sake. And my self-respect."

"How long have you worked here?"

"Three years."

"Have you heard of a man called Wilbur O. Beech?"

"No."

"He's an American." I thought about that. "Maybe not."

"Ever heard of a man by that name?" I persisted.

"Men don't give their real names in this place."

There was a question in her eyes: I decided to stick with Collin. "How old is your little boy?"

"Four." The corners of her lips rounded. "He'll be five in August."

"When does he start school?"

She shrugged. "Depends on where we are."

"You may leave Germany?"

"My work permit expires in September."

"How did you get – I mean, did you have another occupation when you came?"

"Secretary-typist. Before the recession. They fire the foreign workers first. I can't find anything. Rents are up, and –"

"I understand."

"Will you come home with me?"

"You're very direct."

She pressed her lips together and looked away. I felt lousy. "I'm sorry. I didn't mean it that way."

She turned back to me. "I need to talk to someone. I have no friends. Someone to listen. You look a kind man."

"Wouldn't it be more profitable for you to stay?" I nodded toward the men sitting alone.

She bared her teeth in disgust.

"I want to be with you. You're not like them."

"I'll come on one condition."

"What?"

"You'll tell me about Mr. Heimer."

She hesitated. I watched the struggle. Saw the decision before she announced it.

"All right."

The taxi dropped us off in a quiet district of old-fashioned four-storey houses built in connecting neighbourliness.

"The top floor," she said. The house had been converted into apartments. On each landing the names of the occupants were printed on cards in little brass holders. She took a key from her handbag. I wondered if the child was home or farmed out to a babysitter.

"Ah – guten Abend, Fräulein Yin."

An elderly woman with a long skirt and dark blouse came toward us. She had a shawl around her shoulders.

"Guten Abend, mein Herr –"

She had kindly eyes. Not inquisitive. Had she met many men?

"The *Kind* sleeps well," she went on. She took a wool coat from the hall closet.

When she had gone I sat in a high-backed sofa.

Odette called from the kitchen, "A beer?"

"Thanks."

There was a high mantel over the fireplace, jammed with bric-a-brac. On the table a vase of daffodils. A worn carpet on the floor. A playpen was partly hidden in the corner behind the door.

"It's not very cold. I know Americans like cold beer."

She kept her side of the bargain first.

"Heimer's a bad man," she said, omitting honorifics.

"Cheats us out of our commissions."

"And?"

She hesitated. I think she thought I knew a bit about Heimer.

"He's got some illegal side business." Was prostitution legal in Frankfurt?

She was sitting by my side. Hands loosely folded in her lap.

"That's vague," I said.

"Because I don't know much about it. One day I walked into his office unexpectedly, to ask for money he owed me. There was a stranger, a man I hadn't seen about the place before. A big angry-looking man with a beard. Heimer quickly scooped up some little things from his desk and put them in his drawer."

"What were they?"

She raised thin shoulders against her dress. "I didn't get a close look. He screamed at me for entering without knocking."

"Is that why you think he's engaged in some dishonest business?"

"Sounds silly, doesn't it?"

"Honesty means a lot to you."

"I'm Chinese," she said simply.

"Tell me about this stranger."

"Are you a detective?"

"I used to fancy myself being an investigator once," I replied truthfully.

"Well – let's see. He had a beard, was tall and hefty, and had a pink face. An ugly face."

"Did Heimer receive parcels from time to time? Maybe cartons about this big?" I indicated a container about the size of the steel case.

"I don't know." She thought a moment. "I can't

remember seeing anything like that in his office."

"And you don't know a man called Beech? Wilbur O. Beech. Or heard Heimer mention him?"

"No."

Fancying myself an investigator was right: another dead end. I fingered the residual scar on my chin. Then I remembered my side of the bargain.

"I'm sorry about your job. What are you going to do?"

We talked for more than an hour. Rather, she spoke; I listened. She'd had a horrible life. Humiliating. Debasing. I wondered how she'd remained pretty. She leaned against me. After a while I put my arm around her.

"What happened to your other arm?"

"Damaged in an airplane accident."

"A long time ago?"

"A billion years." My body went limp.

She turned to me. "Are you all right?" Her eyes showed concern.

"I'm okay."

She pressed close. I felt her breast against me. I released my arm and lay without movement against the high-backed sofa. Feeling numb. Her eyes narrowed until they became shining reptilian slits. Her lips opened, brushed against mine.

"Collin –" Her breath was warm.

"I – I –" My throat was dry.

Please leave me in the darkness, in the bleak outside I have come to terms with my suffering. There can be no joy – Let me alone in my loneliness.

"Collin – why do you *make* yourself suffer? You said it was a long time ago." Her sweet body scent engulfed me.

I moved away.

"You've lost someone very close," she said, sitting up.

I nodded. Three times.

"I'm sorry – very sorry." She stroked my hand. Although I couldn't feel her touch, I was conscious of the mechanics of it. The doctor had said that was how it would be.

"Make some coffee, please," I said.

We talked about safe things: Frankfurt. America. And Peking. She'd lived there as a child before going to Shanghai. That's where her troubles had started.

"There's an early morning flight," I said. "I must go." I hadn't really decided whether to take it.

I moved toward the door, put my good arm around her and kissed her lightly on the lips. She clung to me. We stood for half a minute, hugging. Over the top of her head my eyes came to rest on the playpen. In it were a toy drum, a tattered Teddy bear and –

I released her, rushed over and stared down.

Near the Teddy bear were a half-dozen colourful plastic toys: miniature models – red sports car, yellow truck, railway engine ...

"Where did you get these?" I demanded.

"Herr Heimer. He gives them to all the girls." She stared at the toys in my hand. "He's always giving them away."

"Always?"

"Well, from time to time. I have some more in the baby's room. What's wrong?"

"Are these the latest he gave you?"

"Yes."

"When did he give them to you?"

"About a month ago."

I turned over the sports car. Moulded bracket for the battery, slot for the electric motor. No identifying name, trade mark, or country of origin.

"Where's Heimer now? I must see him. About these toys. It's to do with a business I'm involved in."

Her eyes grew wary. She took a backward step. "You're some kind of detective. I knew there was something different about you." Conflicting emotions passed over her face.

"Where can I find Heimer?"

"At this time of night?"

"First thing in the morning will do."

She hesitated, and moved nearer the door.

"You were only nice to me to get something out of me. I feel used." Her lip curled. "Just like the others."

"I didn't know you had these in your apartment." I held up the toys.

Her mouth flew open. She put up a hand.

"I'm sorry." Her face softened. "You couldn't possibly have known." She took a step toward me. "Please forgive me, Collin."

"Don't let it bother you." I glanced at my watch. Three-fifteen a.m. "Can I find Heimer at the Cafe Orientale now?"

She shook her head. "He left Frankfurt this morning. After firing me."

"Where did he go?"

She snorted. "You don't think he told *me*. But I know where he is."

"Where?"

"Switzerland. A town called Zug."

SEVEN

There wasn't a direct flight to Zug, so I flew to Zurich and rented a car. Zug was only fifteen miles south, at the head of the Lake of Zug. There was a good road flanked by Alpine meadows and, on the lower slopes, pastures where cattle grazed. Along the northern shore of the lake the green waters riffled under a breeze, and in the distance a blue mountain rose as a perfect backdrop.

On the outskirts of Zug I passed a couple of textile mills, some metalware factories and, surprisingly, an electrical equipment plant. It was a small town. The centre had a mediaeval flavour, and was dominated by a Gothic church. As I rolled by I caught the name Church of St. Oswald. The biggest hotel was not far away. I parked the car and went inside.

"I'm looking for a Mr. Heimer. He's an old friend. I heard he was in Zug and wondered if he might be staying here."

"I'll check the registration," the lady at reception said. She went to a desk behind the counter and turned the file cards.

"Yes," she said. "Herr Heimer is staying at the hotel. He stays with us frequently. Herr Rudolph Heimer?"

"Yes. From Frankfurt." I held by breath.

"That's correct. Room 308. The house telephone is over there."

"Thank you."

I turned away, and hesitated. I hadn't expected it to be so easy. An embarrassing success. What to do? It was twelve-thirty. The foyer was bristling with people; tourists, a few businessmen. I was hungry and, to satisfy stomach and think about my next move, I went into the brasserie, ordered a lager and lunch.

I ate in a detached way, mind working furiously. In my haste to collar Heimer I hadn't thought about my approach. What should I do? Go up to him, introduce myself, and say I was interested in discussing – What? I think I had a subconscious idea he might turn out to be Beech. Crazy thought. Hunch?

I looked around. The restaurant was busy. A man eating alone two tables away glanced in my direction as he tipped his beer stein. He put it down, wiped his lips with a serviette, and his glance hardened into a stare. I stared back. He looked down and picked up his knife and fork. Stop it, Trimboli. You'll imagine a microchip smuggler behind every stein very soon. I examined a rosy tomato and proceeded to slice it.

"Excuse me, mein Herr. I understand you were looking for me."

My head snapped up. Standing over me was a tall forty-ish man with wavy hair. I felt at a disadvantage. I stood, and stuck out my hand.

"Mr – er, Herr Heimer."

He shook it doubtfully, inspecting me with suspicious eyes that had a slight cast. Odette's description fitted.

"Forgive me if I have forgotten. Have we met before? The receptionist said you were an old friend."

"My name is Walton. Anthony Walton. Perhaps I exaggerated. We met briefly in Düsseldorf." Inspiration struck. "At the toy fair. Couple of years ago."

"Oh, really." He squeezed with his fingers the centre of his upper lip, in a thoughtful attitude. "There's a furniture fair –"

"Maybe I was mistaken. Hanover perhaps." There was the big industrial fair.

He looked dubious. "Well – ah." He seemed to want to leave, but curiosity mixed with suspicion held him.

"I think you said at the time you were in business in Frankfurt," I said. "Industrial catering or something."

A faint smile. "Nothing as big as industrial catering."

"Perhaps you said it was a restaurant." His face tilted. "Anyway, I'm sorry to have bothered you. It must be someone else. I was just in town on business and –"

"How did you know *I* was in Zug, Mr. Walton?" The tone was chilly – icy cold chilly.

"Would you care to join me?"

"Thank you."

"Something to drink?"

"Schnapps."

I caught the waiter's eye.

Like his courtesy, my appetite had disappeared. I pushed away my plate. He hunched forward, waiting for an answer.

"To tell the truth," I started to say. "Well – I really *do* have a very good friend who lives in Frankfurt. He often comes to Zug." I looked around, and waved a hand toward the window. "Likes the quiet atmosphere. Crazy about fishing."

"The fishing isn't good."

"So he tells me. Just likes to relax in the boat."

Without taking his eyes from mine, he put the schnapps glass to his lips and swallowed half the contents. He looked at my hands.

"What line of business are you in, Mr. Walton?"

"Air chartering. West Coast – of America."

A ridge of amusement lifted the edges of his mouth. "You're obviously American. You rent aircraft?"

"By the dry lease, management lease, or lease-option."

"Sounds complicated." He took a breath, as if to change the subject back to our relationship. I seized the moment, anxious to keep it my way, delay the inevitable.

"With a dry lease the person who flies the plane is responsible for its operation, care, servicing, and maintenance," I said, quoting the contract. "A management lease is where we provide the airplane, full insurance, servicing and maintenance plus hangarage. A lease-option –"

"I'm sure you didn't want to discuss such business." The tone was sarcastic.

"You indicate an interest."

"I'm not interested in chartering an aircraft."

"Actually, besides looking up my friend here, I'm in the market for some electronic replacement parts for airplanes. Less expensive parts than we have in the States. My friend told me about the electrical factory here."

"They make electric fans, electric irons, the odd industrial equipment." Again, the stony voice.

"I think I can trust you, Mr. Heimer," I said, with all the chutzpah I could muster. "I came to see if you're interested in another source of supply."

"The restaurant business has more than adequate sources." He tipped the bottom half of the schnapps down his throat.

"I'm not referring to the restaurant business. I wondered if you might be interested in an alternative source of supply for plastic toys – miniatures – er, sports cars, trucks, railway engines."

The glass hesitated in its descent to the table.

"I'm in the restaurant business. Why would I be interested in *toys*?" he asked contemptuously.

"There's lots of money to be made. Millions."

"You're quoting *dollars*?"

"Dollars." I wondered if I should have said roubles.

He shifted in his chair. "I think not, Mr. Walton. I'm content to be a restaurateur." He hesitated. "But why did you imagine I'd be interested?"

"The huge profits."

"But *toys*?"

"They have good connections."

"What sort of connections?"

"Sidelines that go with the toys. Children's games, playthings, school supplies – things like that." I tried to recall the list in the Index of American Manufacturers.

"Will you be more specific?"

"Plastic toys with electric motors – and they come with electronics too."

"Absolutely out of my line."

He looked at me sideways, uncertainty holding his features rigid. He was not a good-looking man: the only pleasant attribute was his fine head of hair. His face unlocked.

"I've never thought about moving out of the restaurant business."

"This could be a sideline."

No reaction. I still wasn't sure. Was I misreading the messages he appeared to be sending? I had broken a rule; leaped to a conclusion. Evidence was thin: an address label; a prostitute in his employ seeing – correction, saying – she saw him hide little things from his desk when she'd unexpectedly interrupted.

"It's never too late to change careers in mid-stream."

He shrugged. "As you Americans say, there's no harm in listening." He looked around the restaurant. "But not here. A quieter place."

"Certainly." I crumpled my serviette and put it on the table.

"Not now," he added quickly. "I'm late for an appointment. Unfortunately, I can't see you all day. Unless –" He hesitated. "We meet tonight."

"Name the place and time. I'll be there."

His eyes held a gleam of triumph he couldn't conceal.

"It's my practice to take a walk around the town after dinner. I'll be opposite the Church of St. Oswald at twenty-one hours. That's nine o'clock in American." He gave a slight bow. "You know the church, of course?"

"Of course."

He rose and offered his hand. A sly smile touched the corners of his mouth. He didn't try to hide it. Before he reached the door he looked back. Then he disappeared.

Solid Church of St. Oswald was bathed in light from the street lamps. I walked past the Gothic pile and turned up the collar of my coat against the east wind that blew off the lake and swept bits of waste paper along the sidewalk gutters. There was the side-street corner a little way along, at an angle to the church. It was eight-fifteen. I took a turn around the church grounds. A narrow path led to a perimeter lane and the next street over. I checked my watch again and strolled around the other side of the grounds.

A few cars and a tourist bus glided down the street. There were no pedestrians: sensible people had sought warm restaurants and the fellowship of bars. I took up a position behind the trunk of an old apple tree, and waited.

Twenty minutes passed. A car stopped in the shadows cast by overhanging trees a hundred yards from the corner. Nobody got out.

I waited another ten minutes, deliberately crossed the street ahead of the car, and walked to the corner. I looked expectantly up and down the street, made a point of looking at my watch a few times, stamped my feet, and rubbed my hands against the wind's chill.

A standing target.

But not in a dark room in a factory I'd burglarized. I had a wall to protect my back.

The guttural cough of a car starter, a roar as an engine accelerated, screech of brakes at the kerb. Two figures jumped out of the car, leaving the kerbside door open. But I was twenty feet away and running. Across the street, headlong into the path alongside St. Oswald, pelting toward the back street. Racing footsteps followed, faded as I gained distance. I slowed and looked back. Two men slouched in the glare of a street lamp. One was short and stout, the other tall. As they turned and retreated, the light rippled over the wavy hair of the taller.

"What the hell are you doing in Frankfurt?" Marshall asked. "Aha – the copy of the label I gave you."

"I'm on my way home. Life's too dangerous here. Catching a flight in a couple of hours." My eyes ranged over the clothes I'd taken from the cupboard.

"You didn't get slugged again?" he asked anxiously.

"Once bitten – not on your life. But I have a lead Gilbertson will appreciate. Too hot for me to handle."

He laughed. "Stick to fuel systems. God, I wish I could go fishing."

"What's happening your end?"

"Downey and the other pathologists have identified the cadaver."

"That guy amazes me. How did he do it? The body was –"

"Seems it – he – had had an appendectomy operation a week before he boarded the Novajet. They searched the hospital records in San Francisco and came up with a name."

"There must have been thousands."

"Not with the name they came up with."

"What was it?"

"Raymond Dovosky."

"Next thing you'll be telling me he's Russian."

"I kid you not. This guy's really Russian. Not an American citizen with a Russian name. When I reported everything to Gilbertson he let fly a bit of information –"

"How come? That guy wouldn't give his dying grandmother a mug of hot broth on a winter's day."

"Slipped out. Dovosky's an attaché at the Soviet consulate in San Francisco."

"But he has an American or English first name."

"Probably some sort of cover."

"How do you think he fits into the New York flight?"

"I don't know. You're supposed to be the human mystery investigator as well –" He paused abruptly. "Can you stop over on your way back to the Coast? I've ordered a full-scale review of everything. Everybody on the Go-Team will be present."

"Yes – I have something to contribute. To be discussed, anyway."

"What?"

"When you called me into the investigation you mentioned the radio was silent when they went down. No cuss words or screams. Nothing – all the way down."

"What are you driving at?"

"Captain Phillips didn't call a Mayday."

"Correct. Nor a seventy-seven hundred." A Mayday was a radio distress call: the numerals 7700 were the international code indicating an emergency on board an aircraft, punched into the radar system. On the Air Traffic Controller's screen the aircraft's blip suddenly blossomed into a large blob. "But they were working the fuel management switches to transfer fuel to get a re-light on at least one engine. You established that. They were, to put it mildly, very busily occupied."

"Perhaps it was something else?"

"What do you mean?"

"Sabotage. Beech is an engineer, and everything points to his being an electronics engineer."

There was silence on the line. Then Marshall said, "You've got too vivid an imagination," but there was no conviction in this voice.

EIGHT

"And Doyle brings up the possibility of sabotage, not of the fuel system, but of the radio or radar system," Marshall said.

"I haven't dismissed sabotage of the fuel system," I corrected.

Everybody turned to me.

"What *about* the radio?" Liss asked.

"The radio was silent when they went down. No Mayday. And no seventy-seven hundred."

Liss leaned forward. "Go on."

"They didn't call a Mayday. And nothing on the radio." I looked around Marshall's office where the members of the Go-Team sat close to his desk. "Everybody here knows crews are never silent on the way down."

NTSB tape files were a repository of aural horrors: "Jesus, sweet Jesus – save me." "Oh my God – I don't want to die." "Man, this baby's going down." Curiously, most last words of flight crews, however, were profanities, an evocation of anger because of a mistake. "Oh, shit," were often the last words uttered by a captain before the sounds of impact were heard on the playback of a Cockpit Voice Recorder. I'd read a psychologist team's report on these findings. Its conclusion: nobody in flying thought about crashing. Everybody *knew* they would keep on flying. I certainly did.

"And – no seventy-seven hundred," I continued. "That's understandable because they would have to switch the transponder code, using precious seconds while they worked the fuel management to try to get fuel to the starved engines. But you'd expect Phillips or Warnett would have said *something*." I looked at Marshall. "A cuss word about the flameouts, an order. *Something.*"

"ATC said they heard nothing," he said.

"Have you interrogated the *en route* controller who handled the flight?"

"Dave did." He turned to a puffy-faced man who, in contrast to everybody else, who was in shirt-sleeves, wore a well-tailored suit. His shirt collar, gleaming white, was a size too small. He had a perpetual roll of fat at the neck line that emphasized his stout build.

"Man by the name of Hart," he said, consulting notes. "He was handed over Novajet Flight 101 from Minneapolis-St. Paul ATC." He squeezed a plump finger under his shirt collar to relieve the pressure, an action causing his head to jerk forward like a strutting rooster. He fished out a slip of paper from his briefcase. "The Flight Progress Strip."

It was eight inches long and an inch wide. The strips were used by long-distance *en route* traffic controllers to check flights through their sectors. Each controller had next to his radarscope a tray filled with strips, one for each airplane blip on his screen. As the blip crawled across the scope he scribbled remarks about the airplane's course, flight altitude, requests by the pilot for permission to climb higher, or descend, and the times the blip entered and left his control sector.

At the end of the strip the controller had noted: *Novajet Flight 101 Zulu 01.35.* There was a note, scribbled with a nervous hand: *Zulu 01.37. Blip gone.* Zulu was the international aviation code word for Greenwich Mean Time.

Marshall growled. "Not much here, except time the blip disappeared."

I turned to Jacobs.

"What did Hart say when you spoke to him?"

"Called the pilot on the radio. No response. Tried several other frequencies." He swallowed and dug under his collar. "I asked if he had stuck to the procedure. He said, 'yes'."

Controllers were trained to assume that when a blip vanished the aircraft's transmitting radar transponder wasn't working. The next check was to call the pilot, but the controller never assumed an accident had occurred even if the pilot didn't reply.

"And then?"

"He did it by the book. Turned to the controllers near him and asked if they had Novajet Flight 101 on their scopes. They said, 'no'. And they tried the other frequencies to get the pilot. They had a conference around Hart's scope, then called other pilots in their sector to make sure the ATC radio was working. It was."

"Were there other aircraft in the sector?"

Jacob checked his notepad. "Five. Three Pipers from a flying club over Madison, a DC-10 out of Minnesota climbing through flight level one-nine-zero to cruise altitude, and a Boeing 767, from Detroit, at flight level three-nine-two, bound for Vancouver, Canada."

"Is that all?"

Jacobs nodded. "They called the Boeing first, since he was closest to the Novajet's flight level. Negative – didn't see a thing. The DC-10 also reported negative. They called the Pipers last, but of course they had nothing to report."

"Go on."

"Hart called the supervisor, guy named Everett. He'd seen the activity around Hart's console and was on his way over anyway. At this point the five minutes were up." An aircraft must be more than five minutes overdue at a reporting point for it to be assumed that something serious had occurred. "They called Detroit – Phillips' next reporting sector – and asked if they had Flight 101's blip on their scopes. Negative."

"Then they pressed the panic button?"

Jacobs nodded. "Reported to the FAA Regional Office. The man there called the superintendent in Washington."

"Who called me," Marshall said. "I called my regional office in Chicago and they dispatched two investigators to fly up as soon as Madison relayed the message from the logger who saw the aircraft crash. You know the rest: they reported back to me, and said it looked a fishy one. Then *we* went."

His glance took in the members of the Go-Team crowded into his office. Each was a specialist in some aspect of air-accident investigation. Jacobs was the man responsible for checking Air Traffic Control – how they handled the occurrence when the blip vanished.

"And you know," Jacobs went on, "that Phillips contacted Madison ATC. He gave flight level four-one-zero. Hart instructed him to report this flight level as soon as the aircraft approached Detroit ATC." He snapped shut his notebook.

"Doesn't this point to something odd?" I asked.

"We went over it at the initial inquiry," Marshall said. "But didn't attach significant importance to it. They *were* busy in the cockpit."

I turned to Liss. "Do you agree?"

"It was I who originally raised the question. But they convinced me." His nod took in everybody. "They had the radio transmission switch off and were preoccupied with getting fuel to the engines. No time to switch on and call ATC."

"And with no CVR aboard, we'll never know what was

said," Houston said gloomily.

"Switching the radar transponder to seventy-seven hundred takes time," I said. "But hell, it only needs a flick of the fingertip to switch on radio, an automatic reaction when you've got trouble."

"In any case," Liss said, "How can you suspect sabotage if the radio worked perfectly two minutes before the blip vanished?"

"I have in mind a timing device that would immobilize the radio at the moment the flameouts occurred."

"Too contrived," Marshall rasped. "And too complicated." He clamped his jaws sceptically, then added, "What would be the purpose?"

"To prevent the flight crew from telling ATC they'd had flameouts."

His hand wandered to his protruding ear hair. "Huh."

"We're dealing with a clever and cunning mind," I persisted. "Somebody who's thorough, and knows aircraft systems. And it's a person who knows how to sabotage an aircraft's fuel system –"

"You don't give up easily," Marshall interjected.

"No – and I know *you* don't."

He flashed me a warm smile. "I don't think any of us does."

"And this guy," I went on, "also knows electronics."

"Sounds incredible," Liss said. His eyes raked my face, but there was no scepticism in them.

The office fell silent. The only sound was the angry buzz of a fly banging its head against the window. I looked at the flipover chart at the side of Marshall's desk. Several new items of a routine nature had been added and crossed off. My eyes wandered to the notice board on the wall. It was headed *Go-Team Catastrophic Accidents – Notify*, followed by the names, telephone numbers and pager numbers of the

people who had to be called out to a crash. At the top was
the name of the Duty Officer, Earl Derrigan, who'd
responded to Marshall's decision to get the team up to
Wisconsin when the two regional investigators reported
back after their initial inspection. Then followed Marshall's
name, as Investigator-in-Charge; Howard Bradley, the
stolid-looking man at the other end of the desk – he was
responsible for Structures; Jeff Liss, Avionics; Houston,
listed under Power Plants; Dave Jacobs, Air Traffic Control;
Len Davies for Weather; and Don Ackerman, the man
sitting next to me, was down for Flight Operations.

Near the bottom of the list was George Downey, Human
Factors. I turned and looked at him, a gentle, soft-looking
man with a pear-shaped body, now checking his notebook.
The man had become a legend at NTSB. He had spent more
than half his sixty years working with horrible smashed and
burned cadavers. Everybody wondered how he maintained
his perpetual placidity and quiet self-confidence. He had a
sad face, but it was as unmarked as a child's. It was
interesting how people reacted to grisly scenes: I fell apart
inside; Downey took everything seemingly as a matter of
fact. But he was an experienced and well-known medical
authority who'd come to air-accident work after years of
pathological research at John Hopkins University. I
supposed one eventually got used to dissecting, for
air-accident investigation, hundreds of smashed dead
hearts, stomachs, spleens, and inspecting splintered and
crushed bones. His primary purpose was to establish, with
other medics he directed, not only the cause of death, but to
obtain evidence that would help establish the cause and
sequence of a crash. His evidence was of vital significance in
the medico-legal aspects; millions of dollars of an airline's
money were at stake when relatives of the dead filed suits in
often bitterly fought court actions.

He sensed someone was looking at him, and smiled across with kindly eyes.

"Hi," I murmured.

Marshall suddenly said, "Any comments on Doyle's thinking?" He looked around expectantly.

"Shall I go through the radio system?" Liss asked.

"I think so," Marshall replied. "Huh – I wish you luck."

The plane's electronics had been destroyed on impact. But the smashed bits had been brought back to Turney's labs. I had seen them, but didn't hold much hope for Liss. But a timing device set to put the radio out of commission at the precise moment of flameout could have survived. Mighty Moses, my theory *was* way-out. But suppose somebody had hooked a circuit into the fuel system so that when flameout occurred it tripped a switch and cut the radio –?

"Let's review *your* findings," Marshall said, indicating Bradley. "When the two rear passenger seats were removed it left a space about –"

We went over everything, with each section head reporting. It took a long time. When it was over Marshall took me to lunch. I told him more about my visit to Frankfurt and Zug.

"Before I head back to the Coast I'm going to see Gilbertson," I said, wondering if the FBI had heard of a guy named Heimer. "By the way, I'd like to borrow the Novajet's Maintenance and Servicing Schedule, and the Flight Operations Manual. And do you still have those plastic toys?"

He received me with the warmth and hearty manner of a robot extending a mechanical hand.

"Sit, please."

I looked around the room. A huge Old Glory carefully draped on a staff behind his desk; no other decorations. On the desk, an old-fashioned leather-edged blotter, calendar and pen set. The waste paper container was empty. The room was functionable, and austere.

"What's your 'could be important information', Mr. Trimboli?" he asked, quoting my telephone call.

I told him. Cafe Orientale; polarized opinions about Heimer from two of his employees; my chat with Heimer; subsequent invitation to capture; escape. He listened attentively, eyes never leaving my face, so concentrated he appeared to be listening, not only with his ears, but with his eyes.

"I realized I was getting into something beyond my resources to handle," I concluded with an immodest smile.

That special silence lay heavily on the air. After a minute he said, "I'm glad you realized that in time."

"I hope you found something useful in my tale."

"Indeed. It confirms a point in *our* investigation."

"I'm pleased about that."

His jaw slackened. "We are grateful." He undid the top button of his double-breasted jacket. "Will you describe Heimer in more detail?"

I did, and gave a loose description of the shorter man. "I didn't get a close look."

"I imagine you're wondering why Heimer is important to us."

"Naturally," I replied, surprised that he would tell me.

"I can't tell you *all* we know, but I can tell you that Heimer is the transfer man for stolen United States microchips to the Eastern Bloc. All business is done through Zug. There he meets a Soviet agent. Sometimes a man from Peking."

"I see."

"We know the short man who chased you with Heimer. What we weren't sure was what Heimer did in Frankfurt."

That surprised me, but I couldn't ask directly why such knowledge had been beyond the resources of the FBI.

"But Marshall sent you the label found in the clothing of the then-unidentified body at the crash scene," I said. "Addressed to W.O. Beech, c/o Cafe Orientale."

"We followed it up. It happens to be a contact place used by our man in Stockholm. One of many such contact spots. But he didn't tell us who owned the place."

"Does he play the horses?"

"Why, yes," he said, with no attempt to conceal his surprise. "It was one of his adopted interests in the course of his duties."

"I saw him in action. And he *does* have a way with the girls."

"You're observant." His eyes held a hint of admiration. "He did like women."

"Why do you speak of your agent in the past tense, sir?"

"His body was dragged from the River Main on the Old Sachsenhausen side of Frankfurt two days ago."

My jaw sagged.

"That's why," Gilbertson went on, "I am particularly grateful for this piece of information. We didn't know what Heimer did as cover. Our man, for obvious reasons, was unable to report back in this particular instance."

"Was he stabbed?"

"Shot in the head. Three times."

My bad arm throbbed. Jesus, the way I'd taken Odette home, so casually, my guard down.

"What do you think about the plastic toys, sir?" I asked.

"What about them?"

I mentioned the toys in the playpen.

"Why didn't you tell me before?" he demanded, bristling.

"Not an intentional omission."

I fished in my pocket and brought out a blue van and white ambulance. "Odd there's no identification. No maker's name, no country of origin – nothing."

He shot me a stop-fishing glance, picked them up and turned them over with interest. "They make good shock-absorbing material for air freight," he remarked, putting them on his desk. He re-buttoned his jacket, and stiffened. "How's your part of the crash investigation coming, Mr. Trimboli?"

"Up against a blank wall. I've been over the fuel system many times. Checked the filters and pumps –"

"Don't give me that technical crap again. What I want to know is: was the plane *sabotaged*?"

"I can't confirm it. Some aspects point that way."

"So Marshall says." He pressed his lips together, then said, "So vague. Can't you come up with something positive?"

"We're trying, sir."

He shoved back his chair. I picked up the toys. "Don't you think the key to *why* the plane was sabotaged – assuming it was – is here?" I held up the midget vehicles before dropping them into my pocket.

He got up and stuck out his hand. "Thank you for dropping by, Mr. Trimboli, with your valuable information." In the middle of crushing my hand, he said, "Take care."

Pender reported that they'd been having trouble with *Holy Ghost*. On a routine engine ground test the oil pressure had indicated below normal. He assured me that problem had been cleared up – it had been traced to a slight oil leak in a pipe connection. I tackled the paperwork that had accumulated in my absence. There was a problem with a client who had chartered the Citation for a fishing trip up to

Ketchikan, in the Alaska panhandle, and had damaged a wingtip by running the aircraft too close to a hangar door. I was annoyed that my favourite airplane had been damaged, and assurances that it had been fixed didn't make me feel better. There was also trouble with one of the other aircraft, an elderly Beech C90 King Air chartered on a dry lease to a pulp and paper executive in Seattle. He had accumulated more than three thousand flight hours as a pilot, but somehow had managed to strain the undercarriage on a heavy landing in Los Angeles. At least he'd been honest: the letter said, "I had Inspection at Eaglewing take a look. A bolt had sheared, and has been replaced." I dismissed the matter: insurance would cover.

The King Air got me thinking about Beech, of course. Beech, vice-president of Ling International Import-Export Corporation, Inc., not Beech the airplane manufacturing company. I fished the midget vehicles from my drawer and lined them up in a miniature parking lot on my desk. With a pencil point I hinged up the swivelling ladder of the fire engine, poked the steering wheel of a sports car, and admired the lines of a racing car. After attending to several business letters, I drove home.

As usual, the apartment was silent. I made a cheese omelette, poured hot water into the bathtub, also poured a Scotch, and soaked for an hour, thinking about a fuel system test rig in Washington, a Russian named Dovosky, a guy named Beech, and plastic toys. Specifically miniature plastic toy vehicles.

NINE

I couldn't avoid her. She was the only librarian on duty at the Reference counter.

"You must check out toy distributors too," she said sternly, pulling down the granny glasses.

"I want to get at the source. The manufacturers."

"Not *inclusive*," she said.

I convinced her that manufacturers would probably give me the information. She tapped the computer terminal buttons, catalogue numbers flashed on the screen. It was a long list.

"That's as complete a source as I can compile," she said. She seemed disappointed as she pressed the print-out button and handed me a sheet of paper.

I stared at the list. "I only want *toy* manufacturers."

"That's what I've given you."

"Isn't there a way of refining it to model car manufacturers?"

She shook her head. "No. You could write to the American Manufacturers Association. Maybe they break down their membership by product types, and sub-divide by toys. But you want to know who makes *plastic* toys, and further, who makes plastic cars and other vehicles, and, further," she let out her breath, "who makes miniature plastic toy motor vehicles."

I tried to look contrite. "I am asking a lot."

"That's all right – it's what I'm here for."

I looked at the list again. It would take hours, with no promise of success. It was essential that I re-study the Maintenance and Flight Operations Handbooks, and the thought brought on an attack of a time-is-of-the-essence worry, because I also wanted to pay another visit to San Jose.

"I've changed my mind," I blurted, before she ordered me to the stacks. "Thanks all the same."

I swivelled and strode away, catching a glimpse of a face with an open mouth, and a hand adjusting granny glasses. I went back to my office, ordered *Holy Ghost* to be wheeled out and gassed up, and filed a flight plan for San Jose.

I parked the car in the space marked W.O. Beech. The vacant spot next to it was labelled G. Nordsen. The front door was closed. I swung it open. The entrance hall was deserted.

"Hello," I called.

Silence.

"Anybody here?"

A shuffling movement behind the inner door, then silence.

"Hello," I called again.

I knocked. No sound, so I turned the handle and pushed the door open. Facing me were Mrs. Beech and her son. She held a sheaf of papers in her hand; he had stepped in front of her, body braced in an aggressive attitude. For several seconds we stood facing each other in silence, taken by surprise. She turned to the tall youth.

"I told you to make sure the front door was locked."

His lip curled.

"I knocked but –"

"What do you want?"

"Your husband. To speak to him."

"I told you, he's in Tokyo."

"Your receptionist," I tilted my head toward the entrance

hall, "told me to come back in a week's time. That was two weeks ago." It wasn't exactly true. She'd said to phone.

"She doesn't know what she's talking about," she snapped contemptuously. "This is a private business establishment and you are trespassing."

"I'm sorry."

"We are closed for business."

I stared at her as she clutched the sheets of paper in front of her chest.

"I came to have a few words with your husband. About the Novajet's Servicing and Maintenance records."

"He isn't here."

"Where may I find him?"

"I told you. Tokyo." She looked at the papers as if that was the end of the matter.

"Is the plant working?"

"What –" The question seemed to take her by surprise.

"This plant. Ling International."

"It's not a plant. It's an import-export business."

"Do you import toys?"

Her head snapped up. "Mr. Trimboli, will you please leave?"

"I only asked –"

"It's none –" She stopped, as if an idea had occurred to her. She softened her posture. "Perhaps, after all –"

The boy looked at his mother, as if waiting for a sign. The silence lasted a long time. Then she said, "Perhaps you *can* help me, Mr. Trimboli."

"In what way?"

"Come into the office." Her son followed us into Beech's office.

"My husband phoned from Tokyo to ask me to help him. With the business." She gestured to take in the office. "It's up for sale and he wants me to get a buyer." She stroked the shank of hair. "I don't know what to do."

"How to sell it?"

She nodded. "It's not like selling a house where you call in real estate people and they take care of it." Her voice tapered off.

"Why does your husband want to sell it?"

"He didn't tell me. Why? Is the reason important?"

"Of course. If it's a failing business it will be much harder to sell. On the other hand, if it's doing well, so much the better."

"I understand that, of course." She was silent again. "My husband didn't give a reason. He just said to put it up for sale."

"Why doesn't he come back and handle the matter himself?"

"He's busy. Very busy. Has some important business that will keep him in South-East Asia for months."

"South-East Asia?"

"Singapore, Taiwan, Korea."

She didn't seem to want to hold back on things to do with her husband. I was sitting on the edge of the desk, facing her as she sat in her husband's chair. The boy hovered close, picking his acned face.

"Call in an *industrial* real estate expert," I said. "List the business and the property. You own the property?"

"The business does."

Some business, I reflected. Empty files, empty storage rooms, outdated correspondence. A ghost business. I looked around the office again. Pointedly inspecting the sparse furniture, the carpet – showing wear now that I was seeing it in daylight – and filing cabinets. My eyes rested on the papers she held.

"Are you going through files to prepare for the sale?"

Her fingers tightened on the papers.

"Paperwork my husband asked me to send him."

"Then you know his address in Tokyo."

She hesitated. "He told me where to send them. A Post Office box number. So I need an industrial real estate man."

Surely Beech must have told her. I slid off the desk, and moved away. The kid padded behind me.

"I'm glad I have been some help." I moved towards the door.

"Don't go."

"I'm sorry – I can't offer any more help. Put the business into the hands of a good industrial man. They're listed in the yellow pages."

"But –"

"Yes?"

"How will I know a good one?"

"Stick a pin in the yellow pages." I hesitated before turning toward the door. "Ling International is listed in the Index of American Manufacturers as a manufacturer of plastic toys, games, playthings and school supplies. But the name says import-export. I find that very strange."

"I don't know much about the business."

"What about the toys? Do you make them here?" I indicated the door leading to the big room beyond, and took a step toward it.

"No-no, we – er, import them. They're not made on the premises."

"I thought you had another plant making them."

"They're imported."

"But there *is* another plant."

"I told you, I don't know much about the business."

"Will you please give me your husband's telephone number in Tokyo."

"He didn't give it to me."

"But you have his address. I'll write to him there. Please

give it to me. I'll explain who I am and ask him to tell me where the airplane's records are kept."

Her mouth sagged. "Just a moment."

She picked through a few papers scattered on the desk. "Post Office Box Number F-4103, General Post Office, Overseas Section, Asakusa, Tokyo."

I jotted it in my notebook, making a big show. "Thanks." I turned to go.

"Just a minute." Her voice held a note of anxiety.

"What?"

"I – I really am worried about putting the business up for sale. It's a big responsibility. Could – could you help? Contact an industrial real estate –" She glanced past me and gave a deliberate nod. I swung around as a silver shape arced toward me. The kid lunged. I shot out my hand, grabbed his wrist and twisted. His lanky body whirled through the air and thumped on the floor. As he scrambled to his feet I snapped up the knife that fell on the floor.

"Once is enough." I glared at him. "Into the corner. If you come closer than ten feet I'll carve the pimples off your face." I made a menacing movement with the knife, then snatched the papers from his mother's hand.

"Let's see what you're guarding so desperately."

She reached after them. "Don't –"

I shoved her back into the chair. "Sit down please."

There were several typewritten pages. The first was addressed to Mr. Wilbur O. Beech, Vice-President, Engineering, Ling International Import-Export Corporation, Inc., at the San Jose address. A threatening letter, informing him that unless the bill for the last shipment sent October 21 was paid by April 1st, "appropriate legal action will be taken against you." The letter was signed David Leghu. There was no company affiliation.

"Who's Leghu?" I demanded.

"He owns a firm Ling deals with."

I glanced at the boy, sullen and glowering on the floor.

"How much money does your husband owe?"

"Several hundred thousand dollars. I don't know precisely."

"You know more about your husband's business than you admit."

"I love my husband. Everything was all right until –"

She shut up, leaning back in the chair like a rag doll. Skinny, mute.

"Until what?"

"Until *she* came to work for him," she hissed.

"Angelica Oraschuk?"

Her face said it all: hate, bitterness, suffering.

"Why did you try to kill me?"

"Because you know everything."

"Everything?"

She gestured toward the back room. "What's going on here."

"Why *kill* me?"

"Because I love my husband. I want him back. She's taken him from me. The only thing that will bring him back is this business."

"But your husband wants to sell it."

Her face collapsed. She broke into tears, and looked at me appealingly. "Please help me, please. If we sell the business maybe she'll leave him for a richer man."

"I don't trust you. You and your son tried to kill me."

"I was desperate. Confused. I didn't know what I was doing –"

"How did you know I forced an entry?"

"Steven followed you." She turned toward the boy.

"How did he know I was here?"

"Ask him."

I turned to the kid. He was sitting up, back to the wall.

"Tell me," I demanded.

He looked at his mother.

"It's all right," she said.

"I drove here with my girlfriend. We often come."

"To make love?"

He nodded, picking a blackhead.

"And you saw me?"

Again, a nod.

"What did you do then?"

"Went to a phone booth and called Mom. She said she'd drive over right away."

I turned to Mrs. Beech.

"Why didn't you call the police?" Silly question.

"Because –" She looked around the barely-furnished office. "Isn't it obvious? They might ask questions."

I nodded. "What about your girlfriend?"

"She stayed in the car when Mom came. Then Mom and I came back here."

"Entering by the back window I'd left open."

"Yes."

I rubbed the back of my head. "You tried to kill me with a hammer?"

"No – only make you unconscious."

"And then?"

"We drove to a place Steven knows. South of Redwood City."

"Then you stabbed me." I glared at the kid.

"I didn't want to. But you started to wake up and I lost my head –"

I turned to his mother. "And now you want me to *help* you. What goddamned nerve. I can have you both clapped in jail."

There were many murders and blackmail linked to theft of microchips, Dawson had said. People scheduled to testify in court had disappeared under mysterious circumstances, later found with bullets through their skulls in the underbrush of some country road, or rotting out in the desert.

"Will you help me?"

I glowered at her. "On several conditions."

There was a long silence. "What?"

"You tell me what this business operation covers up. And where these toys come from." I produced the midget vehicles. "And talk about Nordsen; your husband; and this Oraschuk woman."

"You want to know everything."

"Everything."

"Find my husband."

"You already know where he is. Tokyo."

She stared at me for a long time, as if deciding something. "He's not in Tokyo."

I stuck my face close to hers. "Mrs. Beech, can you tell the truth for once?"

"I'm telling the truth."

"But a pack of lies up to now. Where's your husband?"

She hesitated. "Here."

"Where's here?"

"San Jose."

"Where in San Jose?"

"I don't know. I wouldn't ask you to find him if I knew."

"At Oraschuk's place?"

"No. Steven tried to telephone. And been around to her apartment. The janitor thinks she's away."

"How do you know *he's* back in San Jose?"

"That call I got. Telling me to sell the business. It was from downtown. He told me he was back, but couldn't be seen entering the building."

"Why?"

"He didn't explain. I think it's the FBI."

"I'll do my best to locate your husband." No promises to deliver him. "Now keep your side of the deal. Where are these made?" I held up the toy racing car.

"I don't know."

"Seen anything like it before?"

"No – not something Ling imports."

"You're lying again."

"I've never seen anything like that here." She paused, and added with tart conviction, "And that's the truth."

"What about you?" I tossed the tiny car to the kid.

"I dunno. Like Mom says, never seen toys like this around Ling." He turned it over. "Battery-powered?"

"I dunno," I replied mockingly, holding out my hand to ask for it back.

"About Nordsen. You told me his wife's name is Phyllis. Been married only a year. What sort of man is *he?*"

"Greedy," she replied quickly.

"Many of us are greedy. What do you mean?"

"He and Wilbur didn't see eye to eye. Gunther wanted a bigger share in the company profits. And to step up shipments."

"The toy and games company? Or what it covers up?"

Her face came up. There was a long silence. "He was brutally greedy." Her small mouth distorted in a sneer. "He divorced his wife and married Phyllis for *her* money."

"How did he and your husband get along?" I repeated.

"I told you. They didn't. Gunther put pressure on Wilbur to get involved in unethical practices."

A whitewashing job. Protecting Wilbur.

"But your husband is a kingpin in the business, Vice-President of Engineering. Electronics engineering?"

"He's very good too."

"He must know a lot about the microchips he buys for the company."

"I didn't say that."

"But he does buy microchips."

The kid made a movement. I pointed the knife. He edged back to the wall, surly and hostile.

"Your husband *is* involved in microchip theft, Mrs. Beech."

"No – he's in toys and games and the other things you mentioned." She sounded convincing.

"When I came to your house I told you the company plane was carrying a cargo of an unauthorized nature. Do you know what that was?"

She stared at me for several seconds. "No."

"Would you like to know?"

She shrugged. "I don't take much interest in my husband's business. Not the details. If you want to tell me, that's fine."

"Stolen military microchips." I might just as well have said oranges and lemons; her face showed no emotion. "Doesn't that surprise you?"

"I don't know what they used the plane for. I thought it was a quick way to get around to customers."

"The microchips were being smuggled out of the country."

She looked down at the carpet. "I don't know anything about smuggling. But I wondered why the plane was going to New York." She looked up. "I didn't know what was in the plane." She started crying again. "All I know is that life is empty since she took him away from me."

"Did your husband sabotage the plane, Mrs. Beech?"

Her body exploded in fury.

"My husband would *never* do such a thing," she screamed, jumping up and raising her arm. "Gunther tried to kill *him*." She grasped her hands in frustration. "Gunther was the killer. He'd kill for money. Money was his god. He worshipped money. I'm glad he –"

"How did Gunther try to kill your husband?"

"Questions – questions. Always questions –"

"You agreed to answer. How can I find your husband if I don't know the answer?"

She sank back into the chair, and closed her eyes, lips strained in a tight line, shadows falling across her sunken face. She *was* ugly. With her eyes still closed she said, "He was ruthless. Bribed and bullied to achieve his ambition. He wouldn't hesitate to murder –"

"Like you."

She opened her eyes and looked away. "That was different."

"Different?"

"I – I felt threatened. If anything happened to Wilbur I didn't want to live anymore."

"But something *has* happened. He left you. And you're still alive. And, let me remind you, you tried to kill me. I can turn you and your son in for that." It was powerful leverage.

"But you will help me?" she pleaded.

"I said I would. Now tell me about the blonde woman I met in the entrance hall when I visited her two weeks ago. Where does she fit into the Ling organization?"

"That's Angelica Oraschuk."

"Would you mind repeating that," I swallowed. "I'm not sure I heard right."

"You heard right. That's the bitch my, husband ran off with."

Angelica – *with a face to match. And a voice to move a man's heart*. Marshall was right: too much imagination.

"She did his typing?"

"Huh –" The sound was extruded in a mixture of vehemence and cynicism. "She couldn't type to save her life."

"Why didn't she go to New York in the company airplane?"

"I don't know what was arranged. Why would *she* go and not Wilbur?"

"Why indeed? How did she get along with Nordsen?"

"Two of a kind. She worships money too."

"I asked how did she get along with him?"

"She left him alone. He'd already married a rich woman."

"So she turned to your husband."

The tears started to flow again. I allowed a few moments to pass. "One final thing. What activities does this Ling organization cover up? The truth."

"I can't say. And that's the truth."

I waved the switchblade. "Twenty years in jail is a lifetime." I glanced at her son. "He's over sixteen. He'd get life too."

The battle ebbed and flowed. Tears, irresolution, stiff upper lip, more tears. Resignation.

"It's a front for buying and selling microchips and other high-tech equipment. Stolen microchips."

"Where's the real business done?"

"San Francisco."

"Do I have to squeeze it out drop by drop?"

"Not exactly in San Francisco. In San Mateo."

"Let's get it clear. San Mateo this side of the San Mateo Bridge, south of San Francisco?"

"Yes."

"The address."

She gave it to me, with directions on how to get there, which surprised me. I handed back the threatening letter and the others – also not friendly epistles – and wished her luck if she was going to answer them.

"I'll locate your husband as quickly as possible," I added, meaning it. Then I left, taking the kid's switchblade with me. It might come in useful one day – as evidence.

TEN

It was about noon when I backed out of Beech's parking spot and headed from the Industrial Way Estates in the northern section of sprawling San Jose. The weather on the West Coast had suddenly turned balmy, and gaudy-coloured convertibles with their roofs down zipped past me at eighty as soon as I got on to Highway 101. Twenty minutes later Redwood City was off to my left and, on the right, across the salt evaporators on the flatlands, was the glint of Steinberger Slough and San Francisco Bay. I kept a sharp lookout for the bridge – Mrs. Beech had told me that when I saw it "be prepared to turn off at Hillsdale Boulevard. Drive past the Bay Meadows Race Track and golf course, and you'll come to Hillsdale Shopping Centre."

I found it without difficulty, parked, and looked around. It was a big place, the parking lot nearly full, thronged with shoppers. Heading for the adjoining commercial offices I took a right turn, and walked toward a brown building. There was a sign over the office entrance: NB Enterprises, Inc. I'd concealed my amusement when she'd told me the name but now, as I approached, I couldn't resist grinning.

I knocked, entered and stepped into a lake of paperwork and flat-ended cartons. Paper and packing materials were everywhere: on the floor, the shelves that covered three walls, the tops of chairs, a conveyor belt at the back, and the desk of the only occupant of the room. He was a heavy man with a light shade over his eyes, and was in the act of tapping the keys of a pocket calculator.

"Hello," I said, trying not to look surprised. "Are you Mr. Potoroka?"

"What may I do for you?" he replied without looking up.

"Mrs. Beech sent me."

"I see." He continued tapping.

I waited. He jotted on a sheet of paper, fished in his pants pocket and drew out, in a stream, like a conjurer, a tartan-design handkerchief that when flat, would probably measure a yard square. He daubed the pink forehead of his sweaty global face and stuffed the colourful material back into his pocket.

"When's this stupid heatwave gonna end?" he asked, re-adjusting his light shade and peering at me. He had pinpoint, wary eyes, like the eyes of lizards disturbed in the crevices of rocks.

"Search me."

The eyes quickened. "Should I?"

"I don't carry a gun." Switchblades didn't count.

"*I* do." A don't-try-anything-funny voice.

"You won't need it."

"I'm reassured," he said mockingly. "I got a phone call."

"I bet you did."

"What do you want?"

"What I was promised."

"You weren't promised anything."

"Implied, if not promised. I carry leverage."

"Don't kid *me*."

"I don't tell lies."

"What sort of leverage?"

"Sufficient."

"For what?"

"Put two people behind bars. For life. Your boss's wife and kid."

His eyes narrowed. A bulgy lip quivered. "What do you want?" he repeated.

"Where these are used for light-weight packing material." I offered a handful of miniature vehicles.

He looked at them carefully. "These are toys. How would they be used for packing material? And why?"

"To answer your last question first: for light weight and resilience. Ideal for air freight. The answer to your first question is to simply pack them in around steel containers that themselves are contained in bigger wooden crates."

"But why use these?" He handed the toys back. "There are lots of light weight packing materials especially designed for air freight." He waved a chubby hand at the material on the floor. "These cartons and the strips of plastic foam are designed for air mail."

"What do you mail out?"

He pointed to the conveyor belt behind his desk. There was a small stack of pocket calculators at the side. I hadn't noticed.

"Mail order?"

He nodded, and a double chin formed.

"May I see one?"

"Sure." He swung around, took the top calculator, and handed it to me. "Solar cell operated. No battery." Another double chin. "Our hottest seller."

"They do a lot with microchips these days."

"Indeed." The voice was as icy as the reptilian eyes.

"What else do you sell?"

He searched under the pile of papers and cardboard bits on the desk and produced a catalogue. I regarded the colourfully illustrated folder with interest. *PX-9 Cassette: Moon Trip and Guided Tour of the Asteroid Belt. ANG-X7: Space*

Game with Digital Alarm Clock. Government Surplus Miniature Receivers and Transmitters.

"How's business?"

"Can't get the stuff out the door fast enough."

"Where does that conveyor belt go?"

"Back room. Want to see?"

"Yes."

He got up and swung open an inner door. "Watch the step."

"There were two girls in a room, sitting one on each side of the conveyor belt. In the middle of the belt, suspended from the ceiling, was a rack of pigeon holes, containing the items in the catalogue. There were stacks of empty cartons of various sizes alongside, with publicity folders, and a mailing bench with postage machine. The girls looked up as I entered, then bent to their work; consulting handwritten letters, selecting the appropriate items, and stuffing them into cartons.

"Why does the conveyor belt go into your office?" I asked.

"I send through the orders." He pointed to the piles of handwritten letters.

"Just as easy to bring them here yourself."

"I'm a systems man. Like everything automated."

"Why the – er, mess in the other room?"

"You've caught us at a busy time. Had a big rush order yesterday from a department store in New Orleans. Worked all night. I helped out." He motioned toward the older girl, "Elsie's helping with the packing. Usually she handles the mailing."

Elsie acknowledged her abilities with a self-conscious smile.

He returned to his office. I followed. He sat at his desk and yanked down the light shade, a signal saying, "I've shown you everything, now beat it."

I fished in my pocket for the little vehicles.

"Besides being light in weight and resilient, these little things help shipments get through Customs."

"What do you mean?" he demanded, flipping up the shade. A fissure at last?

"If I wanted to show a Customs inspector that a wooden crate was only filled with plastic toys, these would be very convincing." I squeezed a sedan between my finger and thumb. "Besides being shock absorbing."

He snapped down the shade with a flourish. "I've shown you everything here. Now go."

"I'm investigating the crash of the Ling executive jet. For the National Transportation Safety Board, Washington. In the crash we found a steel box containing stolen military microchips, secret microchips, that we believe were to be smuggled to the Soviet Union."

He slowly raised the shade. "This is NB Enterprises. Not Ling."

"Mrs. Beech admitted Ling's a front for buying and selling microchips and other high-tech equipment. She said the real business is done here."

"You've seen what's done here."

"Is Mrs. Beech lying?"

"Sounds like she simply wanted to get rid of you."

"May I use your phone?"

He considered. "All right." He indicated the instrument on his desk.

"On second thought, *you* call her." He had a gun.

He picked up the phone and tapped out a number. After several moments he said, "No reply."

"Let it ring some more."

After half a minute he threw down the receiver.

"The steel box was put in a very big crate. The space

between was filled with the toys I showed you."

"Well."

"But you're not admitting anything."

"I'm not the boss's wife." He patted under his armpit. "I can get rid of you without telling lies."

"Without telling lies – where's Beech?"

"Not telling anything." Thick lips parted in a fiendish grin as he pointed toward the door. "Get lost."

"May I please use your toilet? It's urgent." It was the only thing I could think of to delay.

He hesitated, then indicated with an impatient flourish of his arm the inner door. "To your right." A sly smile ringed his fat, sweaty face. "Watch the step."

The girls glanced up without interest as I entered. To the right, the washroom door faced me. I went in. There was a glazed window behind the toilet bowl, with a spare paper roll and a container of *Comet* cleansing powder on the sill. One of the girls had left her handbag there. It was open. Feeling guilty, I stood on tiptoe and peeped inside.

Lying on top of personal things was a blue plastic model of an MG sportscar.

Like a thief, I picked up the toy and turned it over. The usual moulded bracket for the battery and motor. But, unlike the others, it had a name moulded in the plastic: *Seibu Sha, Tokyo.* Below, in smaller letters: *Made in Japan.*

I tipped the toy back into the handbag, and flushed the toilet. Then I washed my hands and dried them on paper towelling. When I came out Potoroka's figure occupied the step from his office.

"Thank you very much *indeed*," I said, and meant it.

"You're welcome. Now beat it."

Beech's wife must be lying, I told myself for the hundredth time: she may have said he was in San Jose as a false lead despite the fact she wanted me to find him. He could still be in South-East Asia; maybe Tokyo with his mistress. So I rationalized my presence in the comfortable Japan Air Lines 747, with a Scotch on the pull-down table and the kimono-clad stewardess daintily arranging the dinner things.

Sure it was the right thing to do: Seibu Sha would take weeks to reply if I'd written: Japanese businessmen have to reach a consensus with all their colleagues before making decisions. Duly rationalized, my mind, and stomach, were occupied with the satisfaction of dinner. By the time we were on the approach to Narita with the sun glinting on the rice paddies terraced against the mountains, I was convinced I was doing the right thing.

I checked into a commercial hotel near Ueno Park: the prices at the downtown western hotels were at such lofty flight levels I couldn't with a clear conscience nick the National Transportation Safety Board – if my expense account was to be valid – with the bill. It was midnight. I went to bed.

Sunlight pouring into the room awoke me. It was four-thirty – in the morning. Jet-lag had claimed another victim. I took a walk across the wide fields of the park, watched the zookeepers feed the camels and the ponies for the kids' rides, and went back to the hotel as the restaurant opened.

Later, I asked the front-desk clerk, who spoke English, to look up Seibu Sha's address in the phone book and write it in Japanese on the back of my NTSB business card. As a challenge, I walked across the street to busy Ueno Station and bought a ticket from a robot machine. On getting to Meguro Station, about ten miles away on the other side of Tokyo, without getting lost, I congratulated myself on my initiative. It was in reality easy: the Yamate line circled

Tokyo and all I had to do was to get off at the right stop.

The receptionist stared at the card.

"Gomen nasai," she said, smiling prettily, excusing herself and picking up the phone. "Mushi-mushi," she said as the other answered.

I looked around the reception area, and strolled over to a glass case where the company's products were on display. Most were familiar: plastic toys – miniature cars, tractors, railway engines, sportscars and ambulances. There were also plastic toy baseball bats, dolls, toy looms, dolls' houses and colourful moulded airplanes.

The girl stopped speaking, listened, gave a melodious laugh and spoke again, for a long time. She looked up.

"Trimboli-san." She put her hand over her mouth. "So sorry, *Mr.* Trimboli – Mr. Ito will be very pleased to come for you to explain to him nature of your business transaction. He is very good English speaker." She made a polite gesture toward an armchair with lace coverings. "Please to sit down and make yourself very comfortable." She bowed, smiling.

"Thank you very much."

"Would you to like orange juice?"

"Thank you. That would be very nice." I never drank it, but I didn't want to be considered a western barbarian. But I was; I'd misjudged her knowledge of English.

She pressed a button on her desk. A girl appeared, dressed in waitress's apron. The receptionist spoke.

"Hai," the waitress replied with alacrity.

In a minute she re-appeared with a glass of orange juice. I thanked her.

"Mr. Ito will be here in two minutes," the receptionist said with the surety of a radio announcer saying it was two minutes to newstime.

He was a tubby man, with a smile. We shook hands as he

bowed. He gave the impression of being warm and good-natured.

"May I have your name-card please?" he asked, tendering his.

I looked at it. On one side it said Taizo Ito, Foreign Sales Manager, Seibu Sha, with the address and phone numbers. The reverse had Japanese characters on it, which I assumed said the same thing.

"An investigator for the National Transportation Safety Board, *Washington*, D.C." he said, obviously impressed.

"I'm one of a government agency team investigating the crash of an executive jet. We discovered some of those toys," I pointed to the display cases, "in the wreck."

I told him a bit more, and why I had come to visit his company. He seemed in awe that I was working for a government agency.

"We would like to find out who imports the miniature plastic cars and other vehicles into the United States," I concluded.

He pushed out his lips. "Hmmmmmmmmm." The sound reverberated deep in his throat. "I will introduce you to my colleague, Mr. Tanaka. This way please."

He led me to a small conference room. The furniture consisted of a coffee table surrounded by a sofa and three armchairs drawn up in an oblong around the table. On it was an eighteen-inch model of a Heian Court lady dressed in a gorgeous kimono of the period, in a glass case. He picked up a phone next to the doll – the thought passed through my mind of a thousand years historical difference between the two objects – and spoke for a long time. He glanced at my card; mentioned Trimboli-san twice and uttered Washington with emphasis. A few minutes passed before a tall man entered. Ito introduced me; a name-card appeared in the newcomer's hand like a conjuror producing the ace of spades from space.

"Your name-card please, Mr. Trimboli."

I fished in my wallet for another. My loosely swinging right arm caused some embarrassment.

While he read mine I glanced at his. Kenji Tanaka, Foreign Sales Assistant Director.

Ito spoke rapidly in Japanese. But, despite the speed, it took a long time.

"Ah soo," Tanaka said at last, turning to me and nodding. "The National Transportation Safety Board, *Washington*, D.C. I'm very sorry to hear about your crash, Trimboli-san – er, Mr. Trimboli."

"I assume Mr. Ito explained why it's important for us to know who imports the toys."

Mr. Ito's warm smile stiffened. Clearly, I should have put the question to him. I had broken protocol.

"Yes – I understand perfectly," Tanaka said diplomatically.

He sat back in the armchair that was at right angles to the sofa where I sat. Then he spoke to Ito, who pressed a button near the doll. A young man appeared, dressed in a dark suit, white shirt and grey tie. Ito spoke to him, and the young man left. We sat for several minutes in an electric silence. The door swung open and a middle-aged man entered. Tanaka and Ito stood up and bowed. I followed, and was introduced to a Mr. Mori.

"May I please see your name-card, Mr. Trimboli?" Mori asked politely.

I dug into my trouser pocket, pulled out my billfold, and produced another card. His said: Koichi Mori, Foreign Sales Director. As he studied mine his breath hissed through his teeth.

"Ah – soo," he said, taking off his glasses, "National Transportation Safety Board, *Washington*, D.C."

I nodded. "Government agency."

"We are honoured that you visit us. What can we do for you?"

"As I explained to – er," I glanced at the name-cards I had arranged on the coffee table in the order in which the three were seated, "– to Mr. Ito here ..." I told my story, but omitted reference to stolen military microchips and smuggling.

"Very unusual," Mori said, "to use our products as light-weight packing material." He shook his head as if his products had been misused.

"So you see why I – we, need a list of the companies in the United States who buy from you. It may be private business information, but I think you'll appreciate – four persons killed; and it's our duty, as a government agency, to discover the cause of the tragedy to prevent a recurrence." It sounded good to me.

Mori smiled, and spoke in Japanese to the others. He listened politely to what they said in reply. Cross-currents of disagreement, more argument and, ultimately, what appeared to be smiling consensus. Mori turned to me.

"We will be very happy to cooperate with your National Transportation Safety Board, Mr. Trimboli. But we think you will need only the names of our customers on the West Coast."

I thought about it, sorry that I had told them the toys appeared to come from a West Coast supplier because the Novajet had flown from San Francisco. Without realizing it, I had circumscribed my chances of getting all the information I desired because of the peculiarity of the Japanese mind, which tended to see things in a literal way. Tanaka and his colleagues' minds reasoned that since the toys were found on a flight from the West Coast, then they must have come from one of their customers on the West

Coast. There was nothing I could do about it.

"That's very kind of you, Mr. Mori. I'm deeply grateful."

He got up. "Mr. Ito will get the list. Would you like to inspect our factory while you're here?"

"Thank you. But may I ask a question, please?"

Mori sat down again. Ito and Tanaka, who had also risen, re-seated themselves. They turned their attention to me. I produced a toy sedan, railway engine and fire truck.

"Is this moulded bracket for a battery? And this slot to receive an electric motor?"

"Yes," Mori said.

"Do you fit electronic controls too? Controls using microchips?"

"On some models," Mori said. He made to get up. "Mr. Ito will be pleased to show you around."

"One more thing," I said. "These models don't have your company name on them?"

"Let me see," Mori said, looking serious.

Ito and Tanaka gave anxious looks as Mori inspected the undersides of the vehicles. Without a word he passed them one by one to the others, who peered inside the plastic vehicles.

Mori said something in Japanese. His voice expressed annoyance. Tanaka, and then Ito, spoke. Mori turned to me.

"We are very proud of our company name. It appears on every product before it leaves the factory. Our name is on the master moulds. It is moulded into the plastic."

I thought of the blue MG sportscar.

"And we have to put on the country of origin in order to export. Customs regulations," he explained. "Where did you get these?"

"From the crashed plane. They were used for the light-weight packing I mentioned."

He spoke again, in Japanese, to Ito, who picked up the

phone. In a few moments there was a knock on the door, and a man in a white dust-coat entered. He bowed first to Mori and then to the others, but his bow was deepest.

Mori introduced the new arrival. He was the factory production manager, and would like to examine the toys in the laboratory. Would I be willing to lend them to him? I would be pleased to.

"We can probably explain what happened by tomorrow morning, Mr. Trimboli," Mori said severely, giving the impression that his company's reputation was in the balance.

After the manager left, Mori got up, smiled and bowed.

"There's one other question, Mr. Mori."

"Please."

"Do you know a Mr. Wilbur O. Beech? I think he may be an American."

He reflected a moment. "No. Is he in our business?"

"I don't know." I looked at the others. "Have either of you gentlemen heard the name?"

"I – no," said Mr. Tanaka.

"No, very sorry," said Ito.

Mori said, "If you have no more questions, Mr. Trimboli. Thank you for considering our company on your visit. Where are you staying?"

I gave him the name of my hotel. "Opposite Ueno Park."

I expected him to show surprise at a westerner staying at a Japanese hotel. Instead, he said, "Very comfortable." He'd probably never been there in his life: he wanted *me* to feel comfortable. "We will have the list delivered to the hotel at nine o'clock tomorrow morning. With an explanation about the missing words. Will that be convenient?"

"Yes, of course. Thank you very much."

Mr. Ito took me around the plant, making a point of showing me the interior of the moulds where the Seibu name and country of origin were embossed on the plastic during the manufacturing process. I had been over a plastic plant before, but pretended to be interested. Later, in my hotel, I reflected on the meeting and suddenly felt utterly tired. I lay on the sofa. When I awoke, the room was dark, but a phantasmagoria of colours flashed on the ceiling. My God – the hotel's on fire. I rushed to the window: the colours were thrown into my room by the blaze of neon flashing in the Nakadori, the narrow inside pedestrian street on to which my room faced. With nothing to do but kill time until tomorrow morning, I took a leisurely bath, dressed, sauntered down the Nakadori, and entered a restaurant, receiving a few curious glances as I sat down. With the help of a friendly waitress and sign language when I pointed to the menu, the most appetizing food appeared on my table. I mismanaged the chopsticks with barbaric Western non-dexterity, but when I got the food into my mouth it tasted delicious. I ordered more.

The waitress re-appeared. She was delighted I had finished everything.

"Sashimi-ga o-suki-nan desu ne." She bowed and smiled with pleasure.

"Sorry – I don't speak –"

A young man at the adjacent table leaned across.

"She says she is very happy you like raw fish," he said, smiling.

The food still in my mouth suddenly felt thick and unswallowable. I dropped the chopsticks.

"Oh –"

The waitress looked sad.

"Very good. Very tasty," I said, recovering. "Please tell her."

As he spoke her face lit up. She bowed.

"Domo arigato gozaimasu."

"She says 'thank you very much, indeed'," the young man said.

I returned from Ueno Park as the restaurant opened. After breakfast I sat in my room and waited. The phone rang. It was precisely nine o'clock.

"Good morning, Mr. Trimboli. There's a letter for you." It was the desk clerk. "I will send it up."

"Domo arigato gozaimasu."

It was signed by Mori. He enclosed the lab report with the letter, and a list of Seibu's West Coast customers. In the letter he explained that "a chemical solvent had been used to soften and remove all identification of our company name and country of origin of our product. Since we do not know who has done this dishonourable act we cannot bring legal proceedings against the culprit(s). It is very sorry business for us. We apologize most sincerely."

The lab report showed that fifty miniature vehicles had been taken from the production line and subjected to various chemical solvent tests. Results showed that the company name and other identification had been removed without leaving "any indication of their removal."

I glanced at the list. There was a West Coast distributor name, and thirty-one other names and addresses of outlets. The phone numbers had been inserted, and the names of the purchasing agents. I phoned Mr. Mori right away and thanked him profusely.

"When you find the culprit or culprits, Mr. Trimboli, please notify me personally and we will bring action against this wrongdoing of our company name."

"I will phone you immediately. Thank you very much for your kind cooperation. Sayonara."

ELEVEN

I phoned Marshall as soon as the taxi dropped me off at my apartment.

"We got some interesting information from Customs," he said. "After they gave us a negative report on a declaration being made for exporting the crate, they dug deeper. Discovered a shipment of plastic toys had been flown to Mexico some months ago. By Novajet, registration N23456J."

"End of January?"

"Yes – how did you know?" he asked, sounding surprised.

"Griffin re-inspected the fuel filter elements after the plane returned from Mexico. He said it was the end of January. I checked the Maintenance and Servicing Schedule. January 30."

"So there's a possible Mexican connection?"

"Probably a delivery of the stuff from San Francisco. You've told Gilbertson, of course."

"Right away. I guess he's on to it. I called you, but your Mr. Pender said you were out of town."

"I was in Tokyo."

"Get any leads?"

I gave him a brief rundown.

"You're hot on those little toy cars."

"Find the guys who use the toys for packing and we find the smugglers. And possibly the guy who sabotaged the plane."

"You're surmising, on several counts. Dangerous in our business." He chuckled, but there was no mirth in his voice.

"What's doing with the crash investigation?" I asked.

"At a standstill. Except Bill got that fuel residue dug out up in Wisconsin and, although it appears a lot of fuel was spilt, there's nothing conclusive about it. Oh, Jeff reported back. No trace of any timing device to cut out the radio at the moment of flameout. Personally, I think your idea's far-fetched. I hinted that when you were here."

"What's going on at Board level?"

"They're talking about a final report stating the probable cause was fuel starvation of undetermined origin resulting in simultaneous – just a moment, I'll get my notes."

When he came back he continued, "... resulting in simultaneous flameouts of both engines, following which the flight crew lost control of the aircraft."

"That's preposterous – weasel words."

"They said it to put pressure on me."

"An old trick. This Customs man you've been dealing with – is he high up?"

"In charge of a section called Declaration Systems Analysis."

"What's his name?"

"Arthur B. Barnwell. Why?"

"Maybe he can give us some information on other flights of the Ling airplane. Overseas flights."

"What good would it do?" he asked doubtfully.

"I don't know. But it's worth a try."

"I wish you luck," he said ruefully. "I'll give you his number. It's here somewhere."

I phoned Barnwell. It took several minutes of frustration

to get through: Customs came under the Treasury Department and, as I was passed from phone number to phone number, I felt like a pauper appealing for a handout. One woman demanded to know my full name and address in Seattle, which I wouldn't give on the grounds that it had nothing to do with my speaking to Mr. Barnwell. I was sloughed off to another section. I wondered if Marshall had given me an out-of-date number. Eventually a business-like voice said, "Barnwell, DS Analysis."

I gave my name and the fact that I was working with Marshall as a consultant investigator.

"How may I help you?" he asked.

"It occurred to me that we may get a trace on who these smugglers are by back-checking on the prior shipments of equipment, or toys, made by the Ling company. It would be interesting to discover, for example, how they've been declaring the contents of their shipments for Customs purposes. Does your division deal with this?"

"That's our job. Yes, I think we could do that. Unfortunately, it will take time. I'm short-staffed."

"How long do you think it might take?"

"A day or two. We can run a check via the computer, but first of all we'll have to jiggle a bit with the program."

"I understand, and am thankful you can do it. Incidentally, who should I speak to about security at Customs' warehouses?"

"William A. Ogden, Director of Surveillance. He's my number one. Would you like me to transfer you?"

"Thank you."

In contrast to my initial attempt to get through to Barnwell, getting to Ogden took one second. I explained my position. "And I wondered if your division has a system of checking out air freight containing electronic equipment."

"Of course, but we're understaffed."

"Does Customs have legal authority to check suspected smugglers' mail and long-distance overseas phone calls?"

"Mr. Trimboli, I am not free to divulge how our surveillance operates."

"Let me put it this way, Mr. Ogden. If, as consultant investigator to the National Transportation Safety Board, I find out who's been smuggling high-tech military equipment out of the country, would you act on my information?"

"Immediately."

"Then I may be in touch with you."

It was CAVU weather down the coast, one of those crystal spring days when the joy of flying was most intense. The view from the cabin of *Holy Ghost* was terrific, with the Pacific lying under the blue wings like a home-spun carpet on my right and the green mountains sliding past on the left. I kept the altimeter at seven thousand five hundred and the airspeed indicator at one hundred and twenty, and was relaxed and filled with comfort, compensation for the disappointment that Pickers Sales Agency, Inc., of Los Angeles, refused to discuss their business over the phone, but had insisted on meeting me personally.

I landed at San Francisco to refuel, and took off again, setting course away from the coast. The farther south I got the noisier my headphones became. Bakersfield ATC drowned out all others as I was handed off, and shortly after the L.A. tower transmitted a constant babble: a non-flyer would wonder how a pilot was able to distinguish messages meant for him among the jumble. It worked on the principles of a mother being able to recognize the cry of *her* baby among the yells of a score of others in the same nursery. Eventually came a voice intent on reaching *Holy Ghost*. From control at Bakersfield, acknowledging my presence and instructing me to report at my flight level to Filmore. So I did, and flew down the Bakersfield transition leg, where Filmore caught me and repeated my message that I was heading for LAX. I sharpened my lookout. *Holy Ghost* was surrounded by 747s, heading in, a couple of DC-10s on circuit, and several DC-9s and others, but they were higher than we. In a few moments we were skimming at two thousand, and lost more height over cultivated fields. The sun suddenly lost its lustre: we flew over Los Angeles and the smog entered my cabin and exterminated the crispness of the spring I had brought down from the forests of Oregon.

Air Traffic Control took us up, handled us nicely around to the east of the strung-out megalopolis, where the cars speeding along the freeways looked the size of those I had in my pocket. I cracked open the flaps, put down, and stepped with regret out of my little world on to the hard concrete.

Pickers was over in East Los Angeles.

"I'm sorry to put you to this inconvenience, Mr. Trimboli, but you can appreciate our problem." Saunders, the sales manager, opened apologetically. "The competition is stiff out there."

"Perfectly all right," I replied, thinking of the pleasant outing at seven thousand five hundred feet. I told him my tale, but only about the crash and toys.

"We supply the thirty-one companies whose names our Japanese principals gave you," he explained, when I showed him the list. "Plus about double that number between here and the East Coast."

"If I wanted to buy the miniature cars and things in the San Francisco or San Jose areas, which company would I approach?"

"Depends on how many you wanted."

"Several thousand."

"Can you be more specific?"

The exercise seemed futile. How many of the midget vehicles? That depended on how big the crate was and how many crates smuggled out per month.

"I'm sorry. I can only guess. Say – er, ten thousand."

"In that case we'd supply them direct."

I brightened. "Have you supplied such a quantity to a company called Ling International Import-Export Corporation, of San Jose, California?"

"Never heard of them. But I'll confirm."

He called for his sales records. No Ling.

"The biggest order we received from one of our West Coast suppliers, for us to ship direct but pay commission to them, naturally, was for a company named NB Enterprises –"

I shot forward like a released jackknife. "Would you mind repeating that? I'm not sure I heard right."

"NB Enterprises. They're in San Mateo."

"How many did they buy?" I demanded rudely.

"Six thousand. To be delivered without electric motors and electronic controls." He flipped through his sales sheets. "NB Enterprises is our biggest customer on the West Coast."

My arm jumped.

"What would six thousand of these little things look like? Would they amount to a pile this high?" I moved my good arm to the level of my knees.

He laughed. "That's a funny question. They come in boxes, cardboard boxes, packed random fashion. The electronic controls and motor are installed by our customers. We supply everything separately."

"Everything's separate to save shipping costs?"

"That's right. Some customers get requests from retailers for cars without motors and the rest. Especially around Christmas time. We think people like to use them for stocking stuffers."

"What would an order of six thousand packed in boxes look like?"

He shrugged. "Let's see. They pack roughly two hundred and fifty to the box, so a thousand – four boxes. Times six. Twenty-four boxes. About this high. Why don't you come take a look in the warehouse?"

We went, and I stared at thousands of boxes each containing about two hundred and fifty of the colourful toys. I picked through them: every vehicle was embossed with Seibu's name and Made in Japan. Back in Saunders' office, I asked, "Whose name is on the order form and shipping label for NB Enterprises?"

He consulted his records. "Arthur P. Potoroka, Manager."

He leafed through other sheets. "But the latest shipment was ordered by a Ms. A. Oraschuk."

My right arm twitched uncontrollably.

"Here's her signature on the order." He stuck a sheet of paper under my nose. It was on NB Enterprises letterhead. An order for twenty-four boxes of Miniature Vehicles Assortment No. MDL-148 for immediate shipment. And underneath, Ms. A. Oraschuk, in an open hand. I checked the date: March 7.

"Do you know this Ms. Oraschuk?"

"Never met her. She's assistant manager, I believe. Naturally, I don't see every individual order, or meet all our customers."

He pointed to the order form. "Her order was placed with *New Hobbies and Sports*, a retail outlet in San Mateo. We delivered the order direct to NB Enterprises and credited *New Hobbies and Sports* with the commission."

"That's how it works."

He nodded, and shut the order book. "Does that help your investigation?"

"Indeed it does. One more thing. Would you mind giving me a photostat of that order? The one with Ms. Oraschuk's signature. It may come in useful."

He considered. "Sure."

When he returned with the copy I asked, "Do you know a man named Wilbur O. Beech?"

"Yes, he's one of the partners in NB Enterprises."

That didn't surprise me. "You've met him?"

"Once. Why do you ask?"

I told him I'd been trying to find Beech for several weeks. "What sort of man is he?"

He shrugged, "Nice guy," he said without thought. Then he added, "Very astute businessman."

"How do you mean?" A score of other questions formed a line in my brain.

"Likes to strike a bargain – a deal. Take the midget cars, for instance. Insisted on a quantity discount far above the trade discount."

"He bargained with you personally?"

"Came to see me to argue prices. He'd found the toys in *New Hobbies and Sports*, got our name from the manager there, and phoned me. Said he wanted to place a big order and wasn't prepared to pay retail prices."

"When was this?"

He went through his records. "September 30 last year. At least, that's the date of his first order. He must have come a week or so before that."

"Didn't you ask if he was in the trade?"

"No need. I know *everybody* in the business. He didn't tell me what he wanted the toys for, and I didn't ask."

"What's he look like?"

"Tall, nice-looking gentleman. Dresses very well." He thought a few moments. "Well groomed. Bit of a perfectionist, I imagine. Good-looking guy, middle-aged, with nice hair. Now if you'll excuse me, Mr. Trimboli. I've got –"

"I'm sorry. I've taken up a lot of your time. Just two more questions?"

"Okay."

"Have you met this Ms. Oraschuk?"

"No."

"Or Mr. Beech's partner – Mr. Nordsen?"

"No."

It would have been indecent to take up more of his time, so I thanked him, and left, filled with some sense of achievement, but also added puzzlement. As I guided *Holy Ghost* back up the sunlit coast I realized that my journey had not been fruitless: I knew for certain that the miniature toys figured as a key element in the mystery, that Oraschuk was connected with Ling and NB Enterprises, and I'd met two people, Griffin and Saunders, who had actually met a man named Beech. I had almost begun to think he didn't exist.

TWELVE

"But we've tested and re-tested the fuel gauges," I said. "There's no point in going through *that* again."

"Haven't you *any* idea where we should look now?" Marshall's voice sounded tired.

I took the phone from my ear and wiped off the perspiration. The crazy heatwave was still on: Seattle beaches had filled with sunbathers and blossoming Windsurfer sails.

"I'm going through the fuel system for the fiftieth time," I said, glancing at the Novajet Maintenance Handbook open on my dining-table. Several coloured schematic diagrams of the fuel system and its components had fallen on the floor.

"Do you think Griffin had a solid clue when he said the filter element was breaking up?"

"No – he's too fussy. And I think we're all getting frazzled nerves." I turned again to the handbook and test reports on the table. "We've analysed the fuel from the airport pumps in San Francisco. It checked out to specifications. No foreign matter that could cause decomposition of cloth fuel filters and no microscopic particles that might get through a filter and build up. "We've –" I jammed the receiver between my chin and shoulder and scratched the tender place on the back of my head. "I'm going to spend tonight going through everything once more."

"The Board's bugging me. They want a probable cause and a *final* report – and soon."

We talked about other things connected with the crash. He seemed reluctant to hang up, as if being connected with me gave hope. Poor guy: the Board must be giving him hell. When we at last put down our phones I sat with the handbook and diagrams, sipping a pre-dinner glass of wine. I'd put a steak in the oven, on a slow heat as usual, made the salad, and the spuds were simmering in a saucepan.

"Fuel goes through this pipe –" I said aloud, tracing the path with a pencil. "Enters the starboard engine pipe here – goes through the filter there. Bill and I tested the filter. Checked out A-okay."

I took another taste of wine, and sniffed. "This pipe enters the engine here." I sniffed again; something was burning. I went into the kitchen and pulled open the oven door. A cloud of smoke billowed up. Snapping off the oven switch, I flicked the vent fan to full blast, and waved a dish cloth at the smoke. The steak was a cinder with the metal temperature probe sticking up like a distress signal. How did that happen? I wondered, grabbing a cooking scoop and sliding the mess forward. I put on an oven mitt, pulled out the probe, and inspected the head. It had split down the middle.

Too bad. I put the probe beside the mess and shoved the lot back into the oven. Open some canned salmon? Yeah. Later. I went back to the diagrams.

An hour passed while I restudied the complete fuel system, and went over the descriptive and operating notes of all components. The wine glass was empty. I picked up the bottle –

"Mighty Moses –"

I dashed to the oven, yanked it open, and picked up the

probe, the instrument that was supposed to control the temperature of the oven, but had failed. My phone was a step away.

"Is Mr. Ted Marshall at home, please? It's urgent."

A female voice. "Just a moment –" Sounds in the background. Please – let him be in –

"Hello – this is Ted Marshall –"

"I may have hit on something." My hand twitched as I gripped the receiver.

"Never heard you so excited. What is it?"

"I'm kicking my ass for overlooking it."

"For Christ's sake spill the beans."

I spilled them.

"How come we all missed it?" he said in a level voice; he'd been in air-accident investigation too long to leap to conclusions.

I glanced at my watch. "There's a red-eye flight out of Sea-Tac at midnight. How soon can you get Turney to rig up that test again?"

"He never dismantled it. And the Novajet makers said we could keep the plane as long as necessary."

"See you after breakfast."

"Turney's got everything set up," Marshall said, as we swung out of his office and strode to the lab.

"He took the fuel tank sensors out of the new Novajet and replaced them with the sensors from the crashed plane?"

"Yes."

Turney was waiting as we entered the lab. Several technicians hung about expectantly.

"Fill up all tanks, please," I said.

Houston appeared, munching an apple.

"What's this new theory?" he asked.

"We've proved that the fuel gauges are all right," I said.

"My new idea is that somebody tampered with the sensors in the tanks. The sensors that tell the gauges how much fuel's in the tanks."

"Hey – you may have something. Why didn't we think of that before?"

It would have been easy, for somebody who knew, to adjust the sensors to give a false reading. Each sensor was like a metal pencil that simply screwed into the bottom of the tank, where it stuck up vertically into the fuel. The pencil was an electronic device that sensed the level of the fuel and sent electrical signals to the gauges in the cockpit. Very accurate. It worked on the same basic principle as the temperature probe I'd stuck into the meat. Except that, unlike my less sophisticated probe, the fuel sensor had an adjustment nut that was set and locked at the factory when the device was calibrated.

"All tanks filled," Turney called.

"Then let's go." I switched on the computerized simulator set-up and started the fuel pumps. They were wired to the computer so that if the engines flamed out, the pumps would stop.

"I've got take-off clearance from San Francisco," I said as words flashed on the screen.

"Taking off," Marshall grunted in confirmation, finger tip whirling his ear hair mercilessly.

"Climbing on course through ten thousand feet."

"All's well," Houston remarked, leaning over my shoulder.

"At cruising altitude. Switching from internal wing tanks to wing-tip tanks."

"Roger."

It was standard practice, after reaching cruising height, to use up all the fuel in the long-range wing-tip tanks before switching back to the internal wing tanks. A safety precaution: wing-tip tanks could be jettisoned in an emergency to lighten a plane. It made sense to use up all the fuel in them first.

We watched the figures of the fuel gauges on the testbench whirl.

"Is it my imagination, or are we gulping fuel fast?" Houston looked puzzled.

"They're nearly empty," Marshall said.

Red numbers appeared, indicating the wing-tip tanks were running dry.

"Switching to internal wing tanks," I said.

Houston put his unfinished apple on top of the computer cabinet. He scratched his moustache. "Something's fishy."

"Where are we now?" Marshall said impatiently, glancing at his watch. "I've got a meeting with the Board at eleven."

"One hundred miles north of Minneapolis, Minnesota," I replied. "We'll be over Wisconsin in a few minutes –"

There was a sudden silence as the pumps stopped humming.

"Look at that –" Houston said, pointing to the display screen.

"FLAMEOUT No. 1 ENGINE: FLAMEOUT No. 2 ENGINE."

I stared at the fuel gauges.

"Look –"

"Jesus Christ," Houston exclaimed. "Enough fuel left to get to New York *and* the alternates."

Marshall grabbed the phone. "Tell the Board members, 'sorry, I'll be late'," he barked.

"We've proved the gauges are okay," I repeated. "It's *got* to be the sensors."

Marshall screwed up his lips and squinted again down the length of his nose at the words on the display screen.

I looked around for Turney. He had disappeared. Somebody went for him.

"I had to get a drink of water," he explained.

He looked pale. "Are you okay?" I asked.

"Sure – sure. What do you want now?"

"Please open up all tanks and insert the dip sticks."

They removed the inspection panels on top of the wings and inserted the wooden sticks into the internal wing tanks.

"Empty, sir," said the head technician. His companion on the other wing called, "Empty, sir."

"Now the wing-tip tanks, please."

They mounted the platforms they'd wheeled into place at the wing tips, unscrewed the panels, and inserted the sticks.

"For Pete's sake," the head technician called down, withdrawing the dripping stick. Fuel ran over the wing. "It's two-thirds full."

"And yours?" I called to the other man.

"Two-thirds full."

"Get me a worklamp," I demanded, jumping up.

I climbed on to the platform and shone the lamp. The surface of the fuel lapped high up in the tanks.

"It *must* be the sensors," I shouted, climbing down. "Somebody's re-adjusted them."

"Why would anybody –" Houston started to ask.

"To make the crew think it was time to switch to internal tanks before the wing-tip tanks were empty," Marshall said.

"My God – that's horrible," Houston exclaimed. "When they had the flameouts they *didn't know* they had plenty of fuel still in the wing-tip tanks."

"We have to confirm it," I said. "Mr. Turney, will you please drain all fuel from the wing-tip tanks, and remove the sensors?"

While they were doing that we inspected the Maintenance and Servicing Record to see if the sensors had been adjusted.

The records went back to the four owners of the plane. No adjustment.

Turney approached, carrying two sensors. He handed them to me and then, with shaking fingers, picked an unravelling patch on his shabby sweater.

"Good bit of investigation," he said softly, his hollow cheeks seeming less cavernous as he smiled.

"Thank you very much." It was the first compliment he'd offered. I touched his arm. "Thank you for your good work with all this."

I laid the sensors on the workbench. "Small screwdriver, please."

Houston held a sensor from the crashed plane while I slid the protective outer sleeve off the pencil part of the probe. The adjustment nut was near the top.

"Now the sensor from the new plane."

I twisted the screwdriver and slid off the sleeve. The nut was at the lower end.

Marshall slapped my back.

"Thank God you're such a lousy cook," he exclaimed, smiling.

"Who would want to sabotage the plane?" Houston asked.

Marshall shrugged and turned to me. "What about the missing Beech guy? You said he's an electronics engineer."

"A possible suspect. But what about Griffin?"

"You told me he's a perfectionist."

"I can't think of a motive for him to have done it, but he would have had plenty of opportunity when he serviced the plane. Maybe Beech had something on him. Bribed him to sabotage the aircraft to kill Norsden."

"Very imaginative." Marshall's face proclaimed he didn't buy that idea.

"Then there's Nordsen," I continued. "We know very

little about him."

"Passengers don't usually like to kill themselves," he said drily.

It was good to see that the worry lines had vanished from his face. He'd had a hard time: his was the ultimate responsibility for coming up with a *probable cause* of the accident, the Board's legal jargon meaning it was the most likely, if not definite, cause of the catastrophe.

"Cheer up," I said, "you can now write up your final report."

"Thanks to you."

"You'll tell the FBI, of course. Gilbertson will be pleased." I got the impression he suspected sabotage all along."

"Those guys suspect sabotage even when an interstate commercial fruit truck breaks down. They believe it's done to collect the insurance on the perishable cargoes."

"What about this missing woman in the case?" Houston asked.

"Angelica Oras – something," said Marshall.

"Oraschuk. Maybe she's an aircraft mechanic. Fixed the plane so it would crash. Maybe she and Beech wanted to get rid of Nordsen and take over the company," I said.

Marshall laughed. "I always said you've got too much imagination." His face turned serious. "Excuse me, I've got to check something with Downey. Then I'll have to explain to the Board why I'm late for the meeting. At least I've got good news to tell. You staying around in Washington?"

"Yes – Customs promised to dig out a list of Ling Corporation's overseas freighting operations."

"Let me know what you find out," he said, as he hurried away.

THIRTEEN

He was as efficient-looking as he'd sounded on the phone.

"I telephoned you five times in Seattle," he said. "But there was no reply. I assume you're in Washington working on the crash investigation."

I told him yes, and thought it was a good opportunity to see if his investigation had turned up anything.

"Here's what you wanted." He handed me a large envelope with my name and address on it. "Save the United States government postage," he added, grinning.

"This is wonderful – very useful," I said with enthusiasm. On separate sheets he'd prepared information on Customs declarations for consignments from Ling International Import-Export Corporation. I shuffled the sheets. On each declaration under *State Contents*, were the words: *Toys, plastic, model vehicles, playthings.*

"Is this long description necessary?" I asked.

"*Toys, plastic* would have been sufficient."

"They went to unnecessary lengths to deceive."

"Most smugglers do."

"Would such a description arouse the suspicions of a Custom's agent?"

"To some it might. Our problem is that we're short-staffed. It's impossible – nor is it necessary – to check *every* parcel, crate and carton that leaves the country. More

164

effort is spent checking what comes in."

"Drugs?"

"And other illegal imports."

"Where would Ling's consignment clear Customs?"

"Depends on where they're shipping them to. You say the crate found in the wrecked plane didn't have Customs forms or declaration labels. That would indicate, of course, that they intended to do that in New York. But if they're shipping material from the West Coast they could choose from a number of outgoing Customs' clearing points – San Francisco, Seattle, Los Angeles are main centres."

I checked through the sheets Ogden had given me. Ling had cleared Customs for shipments through San Francisco. Nothing through Seattle or L.A. Beech had outrageous confidence in his deceit: he didn't bother to ship through different airports to lessen the risk of discovery.

"Your chief, Mr. Barnwell, has ordered a watch on further shipments from Ling."

"It was arranged at last week's meeting."

"What would happen if a shipment went through under the name of NB Enterprises?" I explained the new name.

"Did you mention this to Mr. Barnwell?"

"No."

"I'll tell him. And we'll add it to our suspects list. Any other aliases?"

"Not that I know of. I'll tell you if I turn up others."

He made a note. "We appreciate this information."

I glanced at my watch. There was a connecting flight for Seattle out of Chicago if I hurried. I thanked him, grabbed a taxi outside his office building, and headed for the airport.

Pender brought me up-to-date on business operations. Things had perked up with the good weather. Every plane except *Holy Ghost* was on charter. Crazy fishermen had wanted to fly into northern Washington State lakes, and some wealthy forest industry executives had arranged camping parties in the woods down in Oregon along the banks of the Columbia. The Citation had been chartered by a group of daredevils to get to a difficult location up the Rogue River, where they intended to raft down the rapids. After he'd brought me up to date, and had gone home to his wife and kids, I put my feet up on the office desk. The lights of downtown Seattle glowed mellow in the warm night. Below me, *Holy Ghost* – it was parked in Citation's open air spot – reflected the distant neon off its wings.

The offices were silent, like the hangar downstairs; with all planes out the mechanics had booked off early. I reviewed progress. Sabotage proved; the FBI informed. In my possession: a history of Ling's Customs' declarations, including a Novajet trip to Mexico; a connection between Ling and NB Enterprises; Beech supposedly in San Jose – but his wife was a liar; Marshall trying to prepare his final, and conclusive, accident report and me with *in*conclusive evidence that Beech was the mastermind behind the whole crooked set-up. Failure in Zug and now – where?

I went over to the coffee percolator, switched it on, and took a trip to the toilet, then jogged around the empty hangar. When I returned to the office the coffee was ready. It was now darker outside, with the tarmac lights doused. *Holy Ghost* lay in the shadow of the hangar, wings and fuselage vague outlines. I thought a deeper shadow merged with the outline of the plane, the form of a figure, but it was only the vague shape of the streamlined fairing over the starboard wheel. The coffee was too hot. So I put my feet up again, lay back in my comfortable swingback, and closed my eyes. I must have drifted off, for a metallic clank jerked me awake.

"Anyone there?" I yelled from the top of the stairs.

Imagination. Had a long day. Jet-lag and all. I went back to the office, took a swig of coffee, and peered outside. A taxiing plane appeared, a DC-8 belonging to World Freighters Airways who had an office down the hall. It disappeared around a corner of the building, and the engines died. I gave a final glance at *Holy Ghost*. Suddenly the shapeless shadow I had imagined detached itself from the plane and moved away.

I threw down the coffee mug and raced downstairs. Crossed fifty yards to the hangar door. I flung it open and dashed outside. The figure jumped the fence between our building and World Freighters'. By the time I ran up the man hurled himself into a car and drove off with tyres screeching.

"A thorough going over," I told Pender. "Flight control system, electrics, radio, engine, propeller – everything."

"He didn't get inside. The cabin doors were locked."

"I know. But check everything. It was a metallic clang, like a tool being dropped."

Pender was thorough. He got three technicians on to *Holy Ghost*. They removed the engine cowl, took out and inspected every spark plug, examined the ignition cables to see if they'd been partially sawn through – an old trick of saboteurs – took off the carburettor and inspected it, removed and examined the propeller, re-installed it on its splined shaft with the care and attention due a new-born baby, and then went over the airframe: wings, tail unit, flight controls – everything that moved and everything that didn't move. After five hours work by his experts, he phoned me at home.

"*Holy Ghost*'s safe to fly. I'll stake my life on it. You need a rest. Been chasing all over the country. Why don't you take a vacation? Weather's great."

Reassuring Pender, a great guy. Blunt, thorough and outspoken. He never worried, never was put off track, and took every day's problems as they came.

"That's comforting," I said. "But I want a radio transponder installed as an anti-vandal device. I think we should do it to all the fleet."

"Aren't you over-reacting a bit?" he said in his placid voice.

"World Freighters had a break-in a year ago. Remember? Two aircraft vandalized."

"You have a point."

"Calibrate them to bleep every twenty minutes when the aircraft are stationary. We can switch them off when we charter out the planes."

"Well – all right. If that's what you want."

"We mustn't close the stable door after the horse – you know."

"Okay. Where shall I install the bleeper receivers?"

"One in our office and see if Security will accept one."

"I still think it's a good idea to take a vacation."

"I'll think about it."

But I didn't. I gathered up all the fuel schematics that littered my apartment – I'd studied one in the bath and it had fallen in and was still drying out on the shower curtain rail – and made a stack of the maintenance and flight operating handbooks to be mailed back to Marshall. The phone rang.

"Hello."

"Is that Mr. Doyle Trimboli?" asked a female voice I vaguely recognized.

"It is."

"You may remember we met –" the vagueness vanished as the European accent came through – "at Ling International Import-Export."

"Yes – Ms. Oraschuk."

"You wanted to speak to Mr. Beech. In connection with the company plane. I told you he was not available, but I promised to give him your card."

"I remember *very* well."

"Mr. Beech is now available. When would you like to meet him?"

"Any time. Er – where is he?"

"At the Ling plant, of course."

"His wife told me he was in Japan."

A pause. "He had to return to the States on important business."

I began to wonder if he had been to Japan: his wife was no truth-teller. The day was nearly done. "What about tomorrow?"

"I'll check his schedule," she said, continuing the charade. She allowed a few moments to elapse in silence. "He'll be in all day. What time shall I tell him to expect you?"

"I'll meet him at the Golden Globe restaurant downtown. For lunch at noon."

"He will expect you at the plant. His – the company plane's documents are in his office." I stared at the aircraft's manuals on my dining-room table.

"Please ask him to bring them to the Golden Globe restaurant. It's near the downtown library."

"Why don't you want to come to the plant?" she asked, making no attempt to conceal the irritation in her voice.

"Ask Mr. Beech's wife."

"I don't understand."

"Let's stop pretending."

"I'm not on speaking terms with Mrs. Beech."

"Mrs. Beech and her son tried to kill me." I made a mental step backward to wait her reaction.

"Why would she want to do that?" she asked guardedly.

"Your question should be addressed to her."

"I told you. We aren't talking."

"Please tell your boss I'll meet him for lunch. Twelve noon. Golden Globe."

"I don't think Mr. Beech will find that suit – convenient."

"Ask him."

"He's not in." She hesitated, figuring how to entice me into her trap: I'd been a sitting target at the plant. "I'll tell you what," she continued, "come to his office and you can go to lunch from there."

I could take the precaution of carrying a gun, except I didn't have one.

"It's a deal," I said, suddenly reversing my stand, reasoning that if I persisted in having it all my way she might call off the meeting.

"I'll tell Mr. Beech," she replied tartly, and hung up. It was easy to imagine her smirking.

I told Pender not to charter out *Holy Ghost* unless it was absolutely necessary. Two other planes would be returning tomorrow so it was unlikely *Holy Ghost* would be needed. I had a good night's sleep, and took off from Sea-Tac for San Jose at six-thirty in the morning.

It was another of those glorious CAVU days. After I got the compass set on course for San Francisco, where I'd refuel since the Cessna's fuel tanks didn't hold enough to make San Jose on one filling, I relaxed. We droned over the forest-covered mountains: off to the left were the peaks of Mount Ranier and to the right the Pacific glinted. It was so clear I could see the coastal shipping like toy ships on a park lake. The main highway south, Interstate Five, snaked ahead, with great logging trucks that gave way to more conventional traffic the farther south we got. We crossed the mouth of the Columbia River, five miles from bank to bank, at Astoria, and pressed on across Oregon. Portland ATC handed me over to Eugene and we were soon over northern California and into San Francisco's sector. I jammed the control yoke between my knees and, with my good hand, unwrapped a cheese and tomato sandwich. As I opened my mouth to sink my teeth into the crispy bread the engine stopped.

I grabbed the control yoke and pushed it forward to stop *Holy Ghost* stalling, held it between my knees and pressed the button. The starter whined, but the engine wouldn't catch, the wooden propeller simply windmilled with the forward motion of the plane. The airspeed dropped to eighty mph and the altimeter was down to five thousand feet. I peered below. We were over scrubland, miles and miles of it, ahead and around. In the distance I recognized the silver shape of Shasta Lake. Directly below, Interstate Highway Five, which I'd been following as a navigation check, filled with huge transport trucks, cars, and long-distance buses.

I switched to the San Francisco tower frequency.

"Mayday – Mayday – Mayday. Cessna Flight Two-One-Zero engine failure. Emergency landing –"

Keep your head – keep your head. Which way is the wind blowing? No clouds: no help there. About two miles away, a small field. With cows. Too far away to see if the cows were pointing upwind – when cows lie down they usually, but not always, face upwind. I tried the button again. The engine groaned. The starter motor complained. I checked the fuel gauge. Below half. Airspeed steady at ninety-five if I keep the nose down. Land on the highway? I banked, losing more height. A solid procession of vehicles in both directions. At several points high-tension cables looped like giant snares over the highway.

Holy Ghost was below four thousand. The centrelines of the highways and traffic direction signs were clearly visible.

We had three minutes flying time. And then, two miles down the highway, I caught the metallic sheen of a sideroad at right-angles to the highway. An empty road leading to some buildings at the end, where a couple of buses were parked. Without hesitating, I shoved the yoke forward to pick up speed and banked toward it, searching for some indication of wind direction: the boughs of trees swaying, smoke from a farm. But no trees swayed and nobody had a fire going. And no cows to test my theory. We glided over the highway, so low I could hear truck drivers changing gears to climb a rise. There was a line of poles carrying cables on one side of the road. We took a sweep across the highway, fifty feet above it – saw faces peering from car windows and a trucker's wide-open mouth – and lined up the dead prop on the sideroad. Cranked down the flaps, and we were flying down a country road, skimming the surface, poles flashing by on our right. The wheels touched, bounced, settled, and we hurtled toward the buses parked at the end of the road.

My God – the first bus was moving toward us, gathering speed. *Couldn't he see us?* I pressed the yoke into my chest, jammed my feet on the rudder pedals so hard I thought they'd go through the floor. As I thought of swinging *Holy Ghost* into the ditch before the rudder became ineffectual, the bus driver jammed on his brakes. *Holy Ghost* slowed, ran out of forward motion, and stopped with the dead propeller one yard from the bus's windshield.

For several seconds the bus driver glared at me. Then he slid his cap back on his head and shouted through the side window.

"Say, Buster – you an alcoholic or sumpting?"

He jerked his thumb over his shoulder. Behind the second bus was a sign.

Welcome to San Basilio Winery. Tasting Rooms Open Daily.

* * *

"You'll have to report it to the Safety Bureau, of course," Marshall said. "Regional Office is in San Francisco."

"But –" It hadn't occurred to me. *Holy Ghost* had become a statistic; forced landings were considered accidents.

"Tell me again what happened."

"Engine conkèd out. No warning – no sputtering or irregular running. Nothing like that. It suddenly quit and refused to re-start."

"And plenty of fuel left in the tanks?"

"More than enough to get me to San Francisco. Christ, I'd better call ATC. They've got my ETA." When I'd filed my flight plan at Sea-Tac I'd estimated time of arrival as two-thirty. If I was late they'd set in motion the aircraft overdue procedure.

"Get on to it right away. I'll contact Medcalfe at San Francisco regional. You know the regulations: can't move the aircraft until an investigator's taken a look-see."

"What about the two busloads of tourists? My plane's causing a traffic jam."

"Can't they back out?"

"The road's a deadend to the winery."

"The what?"

"San Basilio Winery." I looked through the office window at the rows of vines terracing the slopes.

"Oh boy – you're in a fix."

I looked at the other occupants of the room. The manager's face was a mask of frustration. The bus driver, impatiently whirling his cap, glared at me truculently.

"It's not pleasant."

How to break the news to the manager and the bus driver? I started to laugh, deep belly shakings triggered by the irony of the circumstances of my becoming an object of an air-accident investigation. They stared at me. I simmered down. "How soon do you think Medcalfe can get here?"

"I don't know," Marshall replied. "I'll call him right away. Give me your number. I'll be right back."

I put down the phone. They looked at me as if I was a schoolboy caught riding my bike in a forbidden area. "May I borrow your telephone book?" I asked in a pleasant voice.

"When yer gonna move your airplane?" the bus driver demanded.

"Just a moment, please. I have to make an important call."

"I've gotta schedule to keep." The driver stuck his cap on his head, stood with his legs apart and hands on his waist.

I couldn't find the number of San Francisco ATC in the telephone book, so I got it from the operator, made the call, and explained what had happened.

"Well?" the driver persisted, when I replaced the receiver.

"Can't move my plane until the air-accident people have made an on-the-spot investigation," I said firmly.

"Are yer kidding?" He removed his cap, circled his head with it, and snapped it back on his crown.

"I'm not kidding. That's the law."

"You mean your airplane's going to block other buses and cars from using my road?" the manager charged.

"I'm sorry. I'm not allowed by law from moving my plane until a National Transportation Safety Bureau investigator has looked at it."

"But you're blocking *my* road." The manager's voice acquired a shrill whine. "We're expecting crowds of visitors on a day like this. And what about paying for that long-distance call?"

I gave him a ten-dollar bill. He snatched it. "Now get your airplane off my private road."

"Yeah – I gotta busload of people out there and a schedule to –"

"Look here," I said, temper rising. "I didn't land on your

private road out of choice. I had an engine failure." I glared at the bus driver. "I could have been killed, or killed somebody."

"You nearly killed me," the driver asserted.

I drew my lips into a tight line and thumped the desk. The telephone rang. The manager picked up the receiver.

"San Basilio Winery. Andrews speaking."

He listened for several seconds and held the instrument at arm's length in my direction.

"Trimboli here."

"Medcalfe's just leaving. He estimates it's a couple of hours' drive." I replaced the receiver.

"Well –" Andrews demanded.

"The air-accident investigator will be here in a couple of hours."

"*Christ Almighty,*" the bus driver exploded, whipping off his cap and slapping his knee with it so hard I thought he'd ram a hole in the cloth.

"Look here, Mr. whatever-your-name-is. You'd better get that plane off my property this minute or I'm calling the police."

"The police won't break the law," I said, calmer now, thinking how cruel the human race was when bus schedules and bottles of wine were placed ahead of my life.

"What do you mean?" Andrews asked.

"They won't move my plane when I tell them it mustn't be moved until an air-accident investigator has inspected it." I paused, enjoyed a moment of triumph. "They probably know that, anyway."

Two and a half hours later, with several more buses coming down the road from the highway and cramming *Holy Ghost* into an even worse traffic jam, Medcalfe arrived – on foot, and angry: he'd had to leave his car at the highway end of the road because of the parked vehicles. After examining *Holy Ghost*'s undercarriage, engine, propeller, and checking the fuel gauge, and taking down a statement from me, he allowed the aircraft to be moved, but first the bus and car snafu had to be unravelled. It took an hour before *Holy Ghost* could be wheeled through a low gate and into a vineyard.

Medcalfe kindly drove me back to San Francisco airport, and I caught a Pacific Western flight back to Sea-Tac. Pender raised an eyebrow when I walked into the office.

"Where's *Holy Ghost?*" he inquired.

It took a long time to explain. Then I thought about Oraschuk's trap. Later, relaxing with a Scotch, it suddenly hit. A trap within a trap.

"The goddamned bitch," I shouted.

FOURTEEN

Medcalfe called late next day.

"There's sugar in your fuel tanks."

"Would you mind repeating that? I'm not sure I heard right."

"Somebody put sugar in the fuel tanks. It's crystallized in the lower portion of the tanks."

"Can't be. I took off okay, and flew several hundred miles. If the sugar –"

"Whoever did it knows the ropes. The sugar was in a capsule with a timing device. To release it when you were over rough country, I guess."

It took several more seconds for it to sink in.

"I'm sure *you* know what sugar does to fuel systems," Medcalfe went on. "Mr. Marshall told me your background."

Crystallization, clogged pipes, ruined carburettors. The irony was too wondrous to believe. First Mrs. Beech tried to kill me; now Oraschuk. I wondered if anybody else wanted me dead.

"Where do we go from here?" I asked.

"Unless you know who did it, I have to write up a report saying it was done by person or persons unknown. You know the procedure."

"Stall on writing your final report. I think I know who did it."

"Mr. Trimboli, you'd have to be awfully sure before bringing charges of sabotage."

"I will. Where's *Holy Ghost* now?"

"*Holy Ghost?*"

"The nickname for my Cessna."

"At the winery. I had it cordoned off and arranged with the State Police to check on it."

"When will you release it?"

"Right away. We've got what we want."

I thanked him and explained to Pender.

"I'll get a flat-top company to bring it back."

Companies that specialized in transporting aircraft on the ground used long trailers called flat-tops.

"You'll have to take the wings off," I said.

"No problem. But it'll take some time to fix the sugar."

"Replace the fuel lines from the tank to the carburettor, replace the carburettor, and perhaps you'll have to put in new tanks."

"Depends. Leave it to me."

Later, I phoned Marshall and told him I suspected Griffin.

"Take care," he said. "You're working in dangerous company. Why don't you contact Gilbertson?"

"I've thought about it. Maybe later. How are things at your end?"

"The Board won't approve the draft of my final report until I can name the saboteur. And so far Gilbertson hasn't come up with a name."

"What do they think about this Russian corpse, Dovosky?"

"Gilbertson told them it appears he *was* an agent working out of the Soviet Consulate in San Francisco. Beech's contact for getting the chips to Moscow. The FBI thinks he was on the flight to New York to accompany the crate to Frankfurt."

"Why do they think that?"

"Customs have tightened their surveillance and control of

overseas air-cargoing operations. But if you fly on the same flight as the cargo, you can claim the crate personally at the other end by showing your Customs Declaration forms and other documents."

"And reduce the length of time the crate stays in Customs warehouses: ergo – less risk of electronic detection of contents."

"That's what I understand."

We left it at that, with me promising to track down Beech. I spent two days stewing over it, and then decided on action. Fortunately Pender had the repairs on *Holy Ghost* almost completed.

"We'll be ready to do an engine run-up test later today."

I watched from the office window as Pender himself climbed into *Holy Ghost* and started the engine. It fired first time. He ran it until the cylinder head temperatures got up to operating range, and opened up the throttle gradually, with wheel brakes on and two mechanics hanging on to the tricycle undercarriage legs. With a final burst at full throttle, he slowly retarded the lever until the engine idled. It sounded perfect to me.

"I'll get Inspection to do another test when she's cooled down," he said when he came up. "I don't think they'll have any difficulty signing her off."

At midnight I lifted *Holy Ghost* into the night sky, feeling important after hearing the controller tell the captain of the DC-10 red-eye flight to New York to line up behind me. The stars were sparkling, and a honey-coloured moon rising. Dawn came when aloft after re-fuelling at San Francisco, and I touched down at San Jose Municipal Airport in lovely sunshine. I removed the radio bleeper for the transponder from the glove compartment. The mechanic with a penchant for oriental philosophy had stuck another aphorism from a fortune cookie inside the door.

The farther you go, the less you know.

I had bacon and eggs at the airport restaurant, rented a car, and was parked a short distance from the Ling plant by eight o'clock. At eight-twenty a silver Mercedes-Benz swept up the road and turned into the plant parking lot. I focused the binoculars; difficult with one hand. The car eased into the slot marked W.O. Beech. There was a woman passenger in the right front seat. The front left door opened, and a head appeared. A head with wavy hair –. My hand shook as I tried to get a finer focus. Tall – tall and – *Heimer* –. My arm twitched. The passenger door opened and the woman stepped out, a woman in a green jacket and skirt that looked new and springlike, and set off the blonde hair of Angelica Oraschuk. She walked around to Heimer's side, handed him an attaché case, took a key from her handbag, and opened the main entrance door. They disappeared inside.

Heimer – Beech. One person? Don't jump to conclusions, Trimboli. But *if* Beech *was* Heimer it could explain his – Beech's – absence; he was in Zug as Herr Heimer. Not in Japan as Mr. Beech. "My husband's in Tokyo right now," Mrs. Beech had said. Had she covered for him, or had she really thought he was in Tokyo?

I rested the binoculars on the seat, poured a cup of coffee from my Thermos, and prepared for a long wait. Two hours later the door opened. I grabbed the glasses. A man with wavy hair. The car backed out, and drove north. He was a steady driver, and appeared to be in no hurry as he headed up Highway 101. Traffic spread out, and presently I had the back of the Mercedes in full view a quarter-mile ahead. Redwood City was to the left and salt flats and the Bay to the right. It *must* be Beech, I thought, and he's heading for his other business in San Mateo. He turned off at Hillsdale Boulevard and a few minutes later parked in Hillsdale Shopping Centre.

I waited. My bottom ached from sitting. A couple of hours later, in the middle of my second cheese and tomato sandwich, an old acquaintance appeared with the tall man. Potoroka wiped his forehead with the same tartan handkerchief as he rolled his fleshy body into the front passenger seat of the Mercedes. It headed south on Highway 101, back toward San Jose.

Past Redwood City and the huge salt evaporators, cruising down Highway 101 at a steady fifty. The silver car was easy to follow. Other vehicles passed me, got between my Hertz Chevrolet and the Mercedes, overtook that, and another vehicle would overtake me. It was unlikely that the driver of my quarry was aware that he was being followed. We were in Silicon Valley country; near Palo Alto and the other microchip manufacturing centres, home territory for the guy driving the Mercedes.

At the exchange near San Jose Municipal Airport the car took the Nimitz Freeway north, heading toward Milpitas. It turned off at West Calaveras Boulevard, and opposite the Civic Centre slowed and made a sharp turn. I waited for it to pull ahead, then turned the corner. Industrial Way. On both sides were huge modernistic factories and warehouses, with trucks backed up to shipping and receiving bays, fork-lift vehicles trundling between buildings and a constant procession of cars and trucks in the side streets.

The Mercedes had disappeared, lost amid the industrial traffic. I looked around in mild panic, took a right turn, and drove past a row of warehouses. By the time I'd gone around the block three times I recognized the names on buildings. Braking to let a huge truck reverse into a shipping bay, I eased back for a look down a narrow road bordered by windowless buildings. A silver shape was at the far end.

I drove back to Industrial Way, parked, locked the car, and walked back to the alleyway. The Mercedes had vanished again.

A heavy door clanged shut. Walking faster, I came to the last warehouse, put my ear to the cold surface of a steel garage door, and listened. Muffled voices; footsteps. Silence. I ran back to the Chevrolet and re-parked at a strategic spot where I could check the door. An hour passed. The door swung up. A Mercedes backed out. Peeping behind a road map I glimpsed Heimer-Beech and Potoroka as they drove away.

I got out of the car and studied the building. No windows. There was a side-door adjacent to the garage door.

"Hi – looking for someplace?"

A man in blue coveralls was squared off opposite, appraising me.

"Yeah – I was looking for a place to rent. Warehouse space." I peered up at the building.

"How many square feet do you need?"

"Are you one of the maintenance staff?"

"In charge." He was an intelligent-looking man, fortyish, with clever eyes.

"Six to eight thousand."

"Storage, you say. Not manufacturing?" He pointed up the alley. "This section's all warehousing. Manufacturing starts in Section Green."

"Yeah – storage. Must be guaranteed dry and clean. For storing plastic toys."

"Every warehouse in the estate is absolutely dry and clean," he said, with a mixture of pride and indignation. "These people here," he gestured toward the end place, "store plastic toys and games. Been with us a number of years."

"Is that so? What's their name? I know most of the people in the business."

He scratched his chin. "Can't recall now. Private

company. Lease was taken out by a private person."

"Been a tenant for some years, then?"

"Three or four, I guess. Most tenants been here a long time. We've got people who rented space when the estate opened nine years ago," he added with a touch of pride. "If you come back to the office I'll introduce you to the administrator. He'll be glad to show you what space is available."

He pointed to a yellow Jeep in which he'd silently drawn up. At the administration office he introduced me to a compact man who wore a mask of worry.

"Mr. Dunsmuir, this gentleman's looking for space to rent."

Dunsmuir's face perked up. He extended a hand. "What sort of space are you looking for, Mr – Mr –"

"Wallace. Peter Wallace. I'm in toys, plastic toys, games, kid's stuff, you know. Interested in thoroughly dry, airy, warehousing space. About six to eight thousand square feet."

"All our space is dry and airy, I can assure you, Mr. Wallace. This industrial park is only nine years old. Every warehouse is individually air-conditioned with moisture control so you can set your own humidity. We have several tenants warehousing plastic things like building materials and plastic mouldings –"

"The tenant where you were standing," interjected the chief maintenance man, looking as if he was doing Dunsmuir a favour, "is in toys and plastics things."

"Where's that?" Dunsmuir asked.

"The end warehouse on Alley B."

"That's right." Dunsmuir turned to me with his worried face. "Been with us about four years. Good tenants."

"In plastics and toys? Maybe I know them."

Dunsmuir crunched up his face. He turned to the

maintenance man. "What's their name?"

"Can't remember. I think it's a sorta private lease, isn't it?"

"Now you've got me curious," Dunsmuir said, looking even more worried. "Just a minute."

He went to a file cabinet and fingered the tops of folders. He pulled one out.

"The lease is in the name of an Angelica Oraschuk, a businesswoman."

My arm jerked. "Oraschuk?"

"That's right. Oraschuk." He replaced the folder, and smiled a little. "Glad you brought that up. I sometimes forget who's here."

"Would you mind – I mean, how long do you lease these places?"

"Minimum lease is three years with an option to renew for another three-year period. Naturally, you can have a longer lease if you so desire. Would you like –"

"How long did this Oraschuk lady sign for, may I ask?"

"Well – er," Dunsmuir hesitated, worry lines forming cobwebs that fanned from his eyes to the extremities of his lips. "That's confidential information." The prospect of a new customer beckoned. He pulled out the folder and leafed through the papers. "Three years, with an option on three more."

"Thank you."

"I was going to ask – would you like me to show you what's available?"

"Yes, please. Something between six and eight thousand square feet." I paused. "I guess that space occupied by Mrs. Oraschuk's business must be about that area."

"Six thousand, five hundred."

"They use theirs for what appears to be similar products as ours. Would it be possible to see how they utilize their space?"

"I'd have to get the tenant's permission first. I'll look them up –"

"Oh – I thought you'd be bonded and, as administrator, have authority to inspect the premises."

"Only if there's an emergency. Like a fire or something."

"Of course."

He flipped over the flaps of a quick index and picked up the phone. "I'll call her and ask –"

"It doesn't matter," I blurted. "No need to show me hers. Something about the same size –"

"You wanted to see how they make use of their space."

"Some other time."

He shot me a funny look. "All right. As you wish." He replaced the receiver. "We have a warehouse vacant on the second floor at eleven-ten on Alley D that's the size you want. And others farther along. There're two vacancies on Alley F."

He went to a safe, opened it, and took out a brass chain with many keys. "Shall we go?"

While we were standing in the middle second empty warehouse I asked, "Are these premises protected by burglar alarms?"

"Of course," he replied, in the manner of one whose integrity had been questioned. "Electronically, with closed-circuit television on the outside down every alley."

That's how his maintenance man had spotted me, I reflected.

"And our own fire-fighting department," he went on with a touch of pride, and pointed to the ceiling. "Plus the automatic sprinkler system. Yes, I think you'll be very well protected," he added positively.

"You have one more to show me."

"This way please."

He drove me down Alley C and stopped at the end warehouse.

"Is this identical to the end unit on the next alley over? Alley B."

"Yes – the end units are similar."

"In that case there's no need to ask your tenant Mrs. – What did you say her name was?"

"I think it was Orasoshuck – er, Oraschuk." He inserted the key in the door and I followed him into the vacant warehouse. He switched on the lights: there were no windows. The air was fresh and cool from the conditioning outlets on the walls. "Like the others. Well ventilated and clean."

We went upstairs.

"This one has a skylight," I said, pointing toward the ceiling where sunlight streamed in.

"All the end units have them. Don't know why." He shook his head and shrugged. "Some architectural quirk."

"Do they open?"

"Yes, but we don't recommend it. The air-conditioning fits every need."

I looked around. "H'm. This place looks about right. What's the area?"

"Three thousand up and three thousand downstairs."

"We don't need anything too big." I scratched the back of my head and adopted a making-up-my-mind attitude. "We could put our basic stock up here and the faster-moving lines downstairs," I said.

"I'm sure you'd find everything satisfactory."

"Yes – but." I shook my head. "Doubtful about where to put the shelving. Our products vary so much in size. H'm. Very difficult."

"You could put wide shelving around three sides for the bigger items, and narrower shelves for your smaller items here."

I shook my head again, and looked doubtful. "Maybe.

H'm –"

"It is difficult to visualize what it would look like. But I'm sure once you're in –"

"Would it be possible to take a peek – just a quick look around – of the next warehouse over? Alley B? See how *they* handle it. We're in similar product lines."

"Well – highly irregular." Dunsmuir paused, wavering. He tapped his fingers on the wall, and looked around the empty warehouse on which he was losing rent. "Well –" he repeated. "I guess it'll be okay if I accompany you. Just a quick look, mind you."

The first floor contained empty crates. No labels on them. I climbed the stairs after him.

"This is how *they* do it," he said, pointing to rows of shelving.

I stood at the door, toes curled inside my shoes to stop me rushing to lift the lids of the cardboard boxes stored there. Three upturned, empty crates stored in the corner near a door leading to an inside room.

"Looks like they're shipping stock out," I remarked casually, indicating a lidded wooden crate on the table in the centre of the room under the skylight.

"Guess so," he replied uninterestedly. "Well, does this give you an idea?"

"A very good idea." So good I wanted to grab his hand and shake it. "H'm, well, er –"

"Yes?"

I made a negative face. "Very difficult to make a final decision. H'm. Could I have a minute alone to think about it?"

"Sure. I'll wait downstairs."

He went down, and I heard him walking about on the ground floor. I tiptoed to the crates. Since they were empty I could lift them with one hand. I put one on top of the sealed crate in the centre of the room, and with difficulty put another on top of that. I climbed up and swivelled the catches for the skylight. It eased open.

Quickly, I climbed down, replaced the crates, and went downstairs. Dunsmuir looked at me expectantly.

"Well, Mr. Wallace?"

"Yes, it might do. But I'd like my associates to see it. May I come back with them next week?"

"Of course. Will you leave your address then?"

I dreamed up the name of a fictitious plastics manufacturing company and an address in San Francisco, with a telephone number to match, and went back to the car, and killed the rest of the daylight by driving into the centre of Milpitas and eating lunch in a pleasant restaurant. Then I found a hardware store and bought twenty feet of strong thin rope, a flashlight, a hefty pair of pliers, and a claw hammer. After that I looked for tennis shoes in a local department store, found a comfortable pair, bought them, and checked into a motel. While I waited for dark, I tied knots in the rope about every foot. It was a struggle using one set of fingers and my teeth.

Later, the skylight hinged soundlessly upward – no microswitches to trip alarms. I clasped my feet and knees around the rope, gripped it with my left hand above my head, and slowly lowered myself from knot to knot. Since the loss of muscle response in my right arm, I'd developed enormous strength and control by exercising my left. I alternately released and grasped the rope, and at length my feet landed on the sealed crate. Nothing had changed since my morning visit, as a quick movement of the flashlight showed. Crossing to the shelves, I lifted the lid of a cardboard box and shone the light.

Little orbs of gold lay scattered on top of thousands of other microchips. I seized one: MIL-Z-0007. And another.

There were several hundred MIL-Z-0007s buried deeper. There were other tags: MIL-M-3475; MIL-K-89717 and MIL-G-7465. I pulled out my notebook. Some of the numbers jibed. Other boxes were crammed with several thousands more chips. As they trickled through my fingers I wondered how many millions of dollars they represented. Strange gems indeed.

The midget vehicles must be in the boxes on the other shelves. But they weren't: those boxes also brimmed over with chips. I pushed open the inner door. More shelves, more boxes. And a table with a glass tank, like a big aquarium. Instead of fish, the tank contained miniature toy cars and other vehicles, some floating on the surface of a transparent liquid. Cautiously, I stuck my nose over the tank lip: a strange chemical smell. There was a pair of big tweezers on the table. I picked up a model sportscar floating in the tank and turned it over. The embossed words: *Seibu Sha, Tokyo, Made in Japan* were missing, and the chemicals had started to eliminate the moulded bracket for the battery.

"That's how it's done."

The cardboard boxes contained the midget toys. I went back to the other room and got to work with pliers and hammer with the certainty of knowing what I'd find inside the crate. The lid came off after a struggle. And there they were: hosts of the colourful toys. I stuck in my hand and dug down.

A cold, smooth shape. The flashlight revealed the jewel case for the gems: a steel box of the same type found in the wreckage. I used the claw of the hammer to prise off the lid, and leaned forward.

Golden orbs sparkled under the flashlight's gleam. MIL-Z-0007 was embossed on the tags. Dozens were sprinkled amid the heap of chips.

Another surprise: five more steel boxes buried in the

crate, all jammed to the lid with chips. As I sat on the floor contemplating this discovery, the silence broken only by the revving of a truck backing into a distant loading bay, an idea took shape. What if –? After more thought, I left everything, tiptoed downstairs and cautiously opened the front door. The lane was deserted. The lock was a double self-closing type. I took a plastic toy from my pocket, flattened it, stuck it under the lock latch and gently let the door close on it without locking. I walked back to the car and drove off. Aloud, I said: "Try new beginnings. They often lead to success."

Holy Ghost was parked under the stars. I removed the transponder transmitter where Pender's mechanic had attached it to the cabin ceiling, and drove back to the industrial park. I opened the Chevrolet's trunk, removed the wheel jack, and carried it back to the warehouse. Emptying the crate of everything, I laid down a thick carpet of plastic vehicles, rested the jack on it, threw in more toys, and inspected the battery-powered transponder. The timing was easy to adjust; setting it to transmit a bleep signal every five seconds when the crate was in motion, and fifteen seconds when it was stationary. Inserting it into the crate, I switched it on and covered it with toys. In a few moments the lid was on and sealed with muffled hammer blows.

Then came the risky part: carrying six steel cases filled with millions of dollars worth of microchips back to the car. I made three trips, taking two boxes at a time, fixing the front door so that I could get back inside. On one trip the headlights of a truck nearly caught me; on the final journey a security guard called from his patrol car: "Good night, sir." I put it down to the business suit: he'd missed seeing my tennis shoes.

Back at *Holy Ghost*, I placed the boxes on the floor beside the pilot's seat, covered them with an old raincoat, and

drove the Chevrolet back to Hertz, wondering if I should
offer a twenty-dollar bill for the jack. But I didn't: it would
have sounded odd.

"Sorry – lost your jack."

"Oh – where's the flat tyre?"

Too complicated.

So I checked into a motel and went to bed, the
transponder receiver under my pillow giving a stifled bleep
every fifteen seconds. But I was so happy with my day's work
it didn't disturb my sleep.

FIFTEEN

Ogden momentarily forgot his careful bureaucratic voice.

"That's terrific, Mr. Trimboli." He caught himself and continued in a more restrained tone. "We know how difficult it is to bug suspect freight."

"This isn't suspect," I said, "it's *stolen* military equipment. There are military specification numbers on the chips."

"You sound very sure."

"One hundred percent. They're the same type of chip found in the wreckage of the Novajet. I am certain."

There was a short pause over the long-distance line. "I promised to act on your information. Now we can go ahead. I'm very impressed with your action. Where are the chips now?"

I told him. "Did I time the transponder correctly? I set it to transmit every five seconds when the crate is moving and fifteen seconds when it's stationary. To reduce the drain on the battery."

"Perfect. That's the timing we use." His voice was filled with admiration. "What's the range of the transponder?"

"Five miles."

"Any five-second bleeps occur so far?"

"No."

"What's the transponder's frequency?"

I gave it to him.

"Leave it to us. We'll call up the trace team."

"What form will that take?"

"Plain-clothes cars and, if necessary, a helicopter."

"Helicopter sounds a good idea."

"Helicopters are not always a good idea." He didn't explain. "Give me a precise description where the warehouse is located."

I did, and added, "I'll be pleased to meet your team and describe what the crate looks like."

"Thank you. I'll get Customs agent Andrew Parker to contact you. Remain where you are. Give me your phone number again."

The call came at eleven-thirty.

"I'm Parker, Customs," said a flat voice. "I'm in San Jose with a red face. Lost."

"Where are you?"

He told me. He wasn't lost. Only a few blocks away. I got him back on track. Fifteen minutes later there was a call from the front desk. I went to the foyer.

He held a thick attaché case of the type called "brain bags" by airline pilots – the bags contain aerial maps, Jepperson landing charts, current Notices to Airmen and, sometimes, sandwiches if they didn't like the meals dished up by the airlines they worked for.

"Will you come to my room?" I said.

He listened to the regular fifteen-second bleeps. "How far do you estimate we are from the crate?"

"Eight and a half miles on my speedometer. As the crow flies – about five."

He listened again. "Coming in strong." He jerked his head toward the window. "It's the fine weather," he added casually.

"The battery's well up. The unit's new."

"That helps." He looked around the room. "Mind if I smoke?"

"No."

He opened the attaché case. There was a glimpse of electronic equipment as he pulled out a notepad.

"You have your own transponder receiver?"

"Yeah – better set it to the right frequency. What is it?"

I gave him the figures, surprised that he hadn't already tuned in his equipment: surely Ogden had given him the frequency. Sloppy work; I inspected him more closely. Grubby nails, fingers tobacco-stained. One shoe had a black lace and the other a brown. Perhaps it was the way Customs undercover agents worked: appear casual to avoid arousing suspicion. I wasn't impressed.

The bleeps came in louder on his more powerful receiver.

"Well – what now?" I asked.

He shrugged, looking bored. "Wait, and listen."

"Here? In the motel?"

"Sure – I'll check into a room."

"Then you won't need me."

"I guess not. By the way, Washington didn't give me the details of the crate. What size is it?"

"About four feet, by two and a half feet wide, and two feet deep."

He jotted it on his pad. "And the contents?"

"Didn't your office tell you?" I hadn't taken the precaution of asking for identification. "What branch of the Customs service are you from?" I asked firmly.

"Surveillance."

"And your chief?"

He looked at me sharply. "What's that?"

"What's the name of your director?"

"Ogden, William A. Director of Surveillance." He grunted, and pulled out his bill-fold. "My I.D. Sorry, I should have flipped it when we met."

I inspected the card. "It's just that – er." I grinned. "You

don't look like a Customs undercover agent." I ran my eyes
over the soiled jacket and baggy trousers of his grey flannel
suit.

"How should I look?" he asked, without a ripple on his
hard mouth.

"Yes, of course. Silly of me."

"Mr. Ogden didn't give me the details of this job."

He poised his pencil. I told him what had been in the crate
and what I'd substituted to make up the weight.

"Quick thinking," he commented in his casual voice.

"Since you don't need me, I'll check out and head home."

"Where's that?"

"Seattle. Where are the other members of your trace
team?"

"They'll be here in a while." He dropped his notepad into
the attaché case, buckled the straps, and stood up. "I guess
I'll go along and check into a room." He extended a hand.
"Thanks, Mr. Trimboli. You've been a great help."

I went back to the general aviation building at the airport
and wrote up a flight plan for Seattle, with a refuelling stop at
'Frisco. I slid it across the counter to the flight despatcher. At
that moment a loud bleep sounded from my pocket.

"Just a moment," I said, counting to myself. One-
thousand and one; one thousand and two ... one thousand
and five – *b-l-e-e-p*.

"I'm withdrawing the flight plan."

The dispatcher pushed it back across the counter. "Urgent
call, doctor?"

"I'm not –" I waited a few seconds. Another bleep. "Very
urgent," I said, grabbing the flight plan and moving toward
the door. But where to? And why? The Customs' trace team
would be on to it. I sat in a chair, the receiver letting out its
bleep every five seconds. Pilots entering the flight dispatch
office turned and stared. The dispatcher looked over.

"Problem, doctor? Anything I can do?"

"Eh –?" I fished in my pocket, pulled out the receiver and switched it off.

"It's okay. Must be a mistake. It's not for me." I ran for the door. Outside, I switched on the device. The bleeps were louder, growing more clear. I thought of a silver Mercedes tearing down the freeway, the crate concealed in its capacious trunk, with Beech – or Beech-Heimer? – at the wheel and the greasy fat man at his side. Parker and his colleagues in hot pursuit. Heading toward the airport, to load it into a chartered plane. I was seized with mounting excitement. My bad arm buzzed and twitched uncontrollably. Desire to be in the chase tore at my nervous system. The General Aviation aircraft parking lot was filled with swift jets: Sabreliners, Gulfstreams, Learjets. Which was theirs?

But the bleeps faded. I took the receiver from my pocket. In a few moments the sound was so low I had to put it close to my ear to hear the bleeps. What to do? Rent a car and follow? There was a better chase vehicle at hand. I dashed into the dispatch office.

"Changed my mind," I said breathlessly. "Here's the flight plan."

"Everything turn out okay, doctor?"

The dispatcher stared after me as I rushed out, paid my parking fee, and jumped into *Holy Ghost*. The engine temperature needle seemed to take forever to reach the safe operating mark; the tower controller unusually laconic.

"Cessna Flight One-Zero-Niner cleared for take-off."

I rammed forward the throttle and pulled *Holy Ghost* off the runway with the airspeed indicator barely on the take-off indent. Instead of heading north, I struck out south, putting the bleeper on the top of the dash where it would get uninterrupted reception.

"Cessna One-Zero-Niner. What's your heading?"

I told him.

"Your flight plan is for heading three-three-zero. Destination Seattle with a refuelling stop at San Francisco."

"Had to change my plan. I now wish to proceed south." I searched below. We were over limitless surburbia, with an expressway ribboning between the houses and greensward. The bleeps grew louder. In the distance was a ridge of bare-topped hills. I pushed the yoke forward, scanning the traffic.

"Cessna Flight One-Zero-Niner – maintain flight level fifteen hundred feet –"

Bleep – I counted five. Bleep –

"Cessna Flight One-Zero-Niner – you're off course and flying below the designated altitude."

"Roger – Flight One-Zero-Niner has a problem. I'm a private investigator helping Customs Service track a car carrying stolen cargo. I need ATC permission to follow the subject car."

"Just a moment." There were background voices. I peered below. A silver car, cruising in the inside lane. A dark car behind – Parker's? – in the fast lane; dropping in after the silver vehicle.

Bleep – bleep – bleep –

"Cessna Flight One-Zero-Niner. Your request is granted on condition you remain below flight level one thousand feet and obey all visual flight rules."

"Thank you –"

"Roger – have a good day." I smiled at the banality: he couldn't be busy.

Holy Ghost overtook the silver car and the dark car that followed it at a careful distance. We circled and criss-crossed the expressway to allow the two vehicles to catch up. Anybody watching below would assume it was a student pilot practising figure-eight turns.

The built-up area thinned. After five or six miles, the silver car, and its follower – still at a cautious distance – turned off the expressway and headed up a snaking mountain road, where big houses lay scattered amid clumps of trees on the upper slopes. The backyards had swimming pools large enough for a hundred people. Near the top, where areas of level ground had been re-forested, were ranch-style properties, with riding ovals and stables. Several wide gravel roads led arrow-straight through the forest: firebreaks, I assumed. The Mercedes drove along one of these roads and turned through open gates into a long driveway leading to a house standing amid acres of grassy lawns and shrubberies. Then *Holy Ghost* was over and flying above the forested ridge. We came around. I switched off the engine and glided back, silent as an owl, skimming the treetops at a distance from the house. The silver car was parked near a log cabin away from the house. Two men were lifting a crate from the trunk. Then we were past. A glimpse of the dark car stopped in the shadows, outside the grounds – and my view was cut off by the ridge.

I couldn't risk another glide-over. They'd hear me. The forested firebreak roads were deserted. I shoved the control yoke forward, lined up *Holy Ghost* until the tall trees were zipping past the wingtips, and bumped down. Loose gravel shot rearward, zinging up the tail. Then we lost forward speed as the wheels met resistance, and we stopped. I grabbed the bleeper from the dash and stepped out. No sound of vehicles, humans or animals. I turned around to test where the strongest bleep came from, and plunged into the trees.

Bleep – fifteen seconds – bleep –

There was no trail and the going was tough, the ground covered with underbrush that tore at my pants. The trees thinned, and I saw the outline of the cabin, and caught the reflection of the sun off the chromium trim of the Mercedes.

B-L-E-E-P – I stopped, and snapped off the switch.

Silence. A spooky nothingness. I took a step, tripped on a log, and crashed into the brush.

"What's that?" a harsh voice demanded.

I froze, stuck in the brush.

"Wait here," said another voice.

Footsteps approached; cracking twigs. "Who's there –?"

I held my breath.

"Come out with your hands up –" It was Potoroka.

"Who's there?" The raucous voice: Heimer's.

A rushing sound, a form leaping toward me, a roly-poly figure advancing with out-thrust gun.

"Get up."

I got up.

"Jesus Christ – the guy who came to the office. Hands above your head, Buster."

I grabbed my right hand with my left and pointed both toward the treetops. "I don't carry a gun."

"Yeah – so you said before. This way, Buster." He jerked the pistol toward the cabin.

The sly look on Heimer's face spread into an expression of triumph. The cast of his eye gave him a wolfish appearance.

"Did you find your friend in Zug, Mr. Walton?" he asked sarcastically.

"I heard he wasn't interested in chartering a plane –"

"He ain't Walton. His name's Trimboli."

Heimer took a step toward me. "What are you doing here, whatever your name is?" His mouth worked, and he shot an expectant look toward the entrance gates of the driveway. Potoroka jabbed the pistol into my back.

"I was hoping you might change your mind about the sideline I offered," I said.

His face twitched. "What's that –?"

"Electronic sideline. Plastic toys with electronic controls that –"

He whipped his knuckles across my face. "What do you know about electronic toys?"

"A man in the business. Tell your gunman to take that thing out of my back."

He lifted his jaw toward Potoroka. The pressure on my back eased. Heimer glanced at his watch and glanced again toward the gates.

"What's this man's name?" he hissed.

I opened my mouth, changed my mind, and clamped my lips tight.

He pressed his face close, eyes flashing angrily. "What's his name?"

I bit my lip. He grabbed my shoulders and shook me violently. "Tell me –"

I stared into his cold eyes.

"Wilbur O. *Beech* –"

A glimpse of a fist sweeping up, a lightning flash behind my eyes, my knees lost all feeling, and the odour of dead leaves filled my nostrils. Then everything faded.

Thunder reverberated through my skull; lightning strokes cracked against my temples; voices shouted, echoed in cavernous chambers. I put my hand over my forehead to shut out the pain, and opened my eyes. I was lying on a couch, in a room with walls of semi-circular logs. Walking unsteadily to the window, I peeked between the drapes. A Lincoln Continental was drawn up next to the Mercedes. Heimer and Potoroka were shaking hands with three other men. A woman clambered from the back of the Lincoln and slammed the door. A woman clutching blonde hair as she turned to Heimer. Oraschuk.

The window catch was screwed down: double glazing. I

went to the door. It rattled against the lock. In panic, I felt inside my pocket. Ah – the receiver was intact. I slid the button to On.

B-L-E-E-P –

I switched off. Footsteps clomped into the cabin.

"Big shipment." A new voice.

"As arranged."

"Well cushioned, I hope."

"We've never had a failure." Potoroka.

"Sign these papers." Heimer.

"Just a moment." Another voice, authoritative. "Run the metal detector over it."

"No need to." Heimer sounded anxious. "Everything's in order."

"To be safe –"

"I packed it myself. What's the problem? You never pay until it gets to Moscow."

"Make sure Customs doesn't get a buzz. Mike, bring the detector."

Footsteps sounded in the next room. Opening and banging of a door. I turned to the window. A man went to the Lincoln and returned with a metal box.

"Plug it in."

I pressed my ear to the door. There was no sound. Then: "A-okay. Great how that plastic stuff insulates the acoustics. Drowns out metal."

"Trick is to use a lot," Heimer said. "Hurry – get it in your car and be on your way."

I tiptoed to the window. They carried the crate toward the Lincoln. A man opened the trunk –

Flumph – flumph – flumph – The sound of powerful engines roared above the treetops. Rotor blades flashed in the sunlight. The men carrying the crate looked up, mouths gaping. The helicopter swiftly descended, fifty yards from the cabin. The wheels bounced, doors flew open, men grasping guns leaped to the ground under dying rotor blades. A dark car dashed across the open space, slithering on the grass. It jerked to a stop. A man jumped out – Parker – gun in hand, tails of his soiled flannel jacket flying, and rushed towards the men lugging the crate. They dropped it and fled for the forest.

Parker yelled, and pointed his gun. A shot ricocheted through the clearing.

In a few seconds it was all over. Potoroka, waddling toward the trees, fat legs flying like windmills, fell on his face and was rounded up by one of the Customs men. His companions turned and shoved their hands skyward. But Heimer and Oraschuk rushed back to the cabin, threw themselves in, and slammed the front door. Heavy bolts rammed shut. A key rattled in the door of my room.

"Get – in – here," Heimer panted, pointing the pistol.

"Hello, Miss Oraschuk," I said as sweetly as I could. My knees felt buttery.

"*You –*" she cried contemptuously. Her lips recoiled as if to spit at me.

"Shut up," Heimer snapped. He shoved me toward the window. "Show your face."

I drew back. "They'll shoot me."

"A good idea," Oraschuk sneered.

"Show yourself," Heimer commanded. He was a big man. His body hefted against me.

There was banging on the door.

"Heimer – come out with your hands up."

"I have a hostage," Heimer shouted. "I won't hesitate to shoot him." He levelled the gun at my heart. "A Mr. Walton – or Trimboli. Take your pick."

Silence outside.

"Tell your men to withdraw. To give us safe conduct."

The silence was like a pall of condemnation. It seemed to

unnerve him. The pistol shook.

"I'll give you one more chance," he hissed at me. "Show your face at the window –"

I stared at the dark opening at the end of the gun, at the finger tensed on the trigger. And then, suddenly, fear evaporated: *Anne and Peter and Sarah ... God ... give me strength ... to end the misery ... so simple ... one second of pain and it'll be over ... the years of suffering ahead ... they'll all vanish ... in a second ... trade in a second of anguish for ...*

I slowly raised my eyes and looked into Heimer's. They glittered with a mixture of triumph, and fear. As I outstared him, a puzzled look lay in their depths. My eyes descended. The finger curling around the trigger relaxed.

"Gott in heaven –" The gun muzzle dropped.

"Kill him," Oraschuk said.

"We need him as a hostage."

"You fool, Wilbur. He's laughing at you. He knows you won't kill him."

"I can't shoot in cold blood."

"You killed Gunther without a thought about –"

"That was different. I wasn't there when it happened."

"You arranged it. What's the difference?"

"Shut up."

Oraschuk's lip curled. "If you'd listened to Gunther we wouldn't be in this mess."

"Shut up," Heimer repeated, shooting a glance at me.

"Gunther told you to stop hurrying deliveries." Oraschuk put her hands on her waist. "But no – you couldn't wait. You were greedy. You had to get rid of him, you said, even if it meant losing a million-dollar shipment *and* the company plane –"

"The insurance will –"

"Come out the door with your hands up," Parker yelled. "I'll count up to three."

The pistol jabbed at my chest. "Over to the window – quick."

"O-n-e –"

I let my body slump. Heimer shoved me. I was a rubber stanchion, flippy-floppy.

"T-w-o –"

My toes curled against the soles of my shoes.

"T-h-r-e-e –" There was a movement against the side of the cabin.

"Move –" Heimer hissed.

Oraschuk rushed forward. "Give *me* the –"

Heimer jerked the gun into the air. I lowered my head, and charged. The gun clattered on the floor. Oraschuk, springing like a leopard, grabbed it. I stamped on her hand. She screamed. There were crashing noises, shouts, bodies in flying tackles zipping past –

"You okay, Trimboli?"

"I think –" I flopped into a chair, dizzy, trying to focus my eyes. Parker and another Customs man gripped Heimer; snap of handcuffs; Oraschuk's harsh voice protesting; men telling her it was all over.

A skinny man stepped into the cabin. He looked at me with the expression of a school principal annoyed by a misbehaving student.

"What are *you* doing here?" he demanded. His face softened. "Congratulations – hiding that transponder transmitter in the crate was a brilliant idea."

"Why didn't they simply drive to some rendezvous in San Francisco and hand over the crate to the Soviet agents?" I asked between sips of coffee.

"Too risky," Bony replied.

We were sitting around the main room of the cabin. Handcuffed Heimer and Oraschuk were in the room where they'd locked me.

"They could have air-freighted it the usual way." I rubbed my scalp. "It would have got to Frankfurt quite –"

"It wouldn't," Parker interjected. "We have every air freight terminal handling flights to Europe under special surveillance. We're training more agents to cover every terminal in the country to *all* destinations."

I turned to Bony. "Why are *you* here, sir?"

"We've been working closely with Customs." He didn't seem to mind the direct question.

I nodded toward the other room. "Who's that guy? Beech or Heimer?"

"Heimer in Frankfurt." His sunken cheeks formed a surprise smile. "And in Zug. But he's Beech in San Jose."

"I wasn't sure. But it fits."

"One more thing," I said, turning back to Bony. "Why did the Novajet fly down to Mexico?"

"We made things tough for them on the West Coast." He nodded at Parker. "They tried one shipment through Mexico City. We warned Mexican Customs, who put the clamps on Heimer, but he got away with the shipment and flew it back to San Jose. Later, they decided to fly it to New York for onward transfer to Frankfurt by scheduled airline. With the Soviet agent Dovosky travelling on the same flight so he could claim it without delay at the other end."

I put down my cup and pointed to the crate around which we were sitting.

"By the way," I said to Parker. "Would the United States Customs mind if I opened it?"

Parker looked worried. "What for? You said you removed the six containers of microchips."

"Well – after all, it's *my* transponder."

He grinned. "You'll need a claw hammer."

Someone spoke to a man at the doorway. In a few moments he reappeared with a hammer.

I stood up and pretended to be reluctant to open the crate.

"I'm at a disadvantage. My bad arm."

"You opened it to take out the containers –"

"I'd like Mr. Wilbur O. Beech-Heimer to open it."

There was a moment of silence. Then everybody laughed.

"Good idea," Parker said.

He drew his gun while Beech-Heimer pulled out the nails. I'd driven them in hard, and one of Parker's men had to help. They lifted off the lid. Miniature plastic vehicles tumbled on to the floor. The Customs man searched around with his hand.

"Your transponder transmitter, sir," he said, handing me the device.

Beech-Heimer's face distorted with rage.

"As an electronics expert, I thought you'd appreciate that," I taunted. "Would you please dig deeper into *your* crate?"

He stared at the heap of toys lining the crate. Oraschuk, held by an agent, watched from the doorway of the adjoining room. Heimer dug his arm up to the elbow in the tiny vehicles. He froze as his fingers felt something solid.

"Please bring out what you've found," I said.

He hesitated.

"I promise it won't cause engine failure, stab you, explode or burn."

An avalanche of the little plastic vehicles tumbled on the floor as his arm came out. He stared at the jack uncomprehendingly.

"You fool, Wilbur," Oraschuk screamed. "You god-damned fool. They tricked you."

He grasped the jack handle and struck out in my direction.

"Drop it –" Parker shoved the muzzle of his gun into Heimer's face.

"Take them away," Parker said.

I picked up the jack. "Would somebody please help me find my way back to *Holy Ghost*? I have to return this to

Hertz." I addressed Parker. "And besides, you want the chips back."

It took a little explaining.

Aloft in the starry night, with *Holy Ghost*'s engine purring homeward, in my little world of leather seats and soft instrument lights, I felt strangely contented-sad. The lights of Tacoma and then, presently, Seattle, edged up over the dashboard, stretching out to welcome me. But my feeling of achievement was mixed with the sadness of the prospect of opening the door of my lonely apartment, switching on the TV for company, searching in the fridge for something to eat, and sorting out the accumulated mail.

I got it over with. Then called Marshall at home. It was seven in the morning in Washington.

"The guy's name you need for your Novajet *final* report is Wilbur Oliver Beech-Heimer."

"Beech-Heimer?"

I explained.

"Oh, incidentally, Gilbertson called," he said. "They took Griffin in for questioning in San Francisco. It seems certain he's implicated in stealing chips. Now they've got Beech – er, Beech-Heimer, they'll put the pressure on. Gilbertson said evidence points to Beech-Heimer having something on Griffin and blackmailing him to sabotage the plane."

I thought about the prowler I'd chased from *Holy Ghost*. That, too, was a safe bet: Griffin. Put up to it by Oraschuk. But sugar in the fuel tank? He could have devised a more sophisticated method. On the other hand, he had to do it in a hurry.

"How come there was a last-minute change of passengers before the Novajet took off for New York?" Marshall inquired.

"I asked Bony about –"

"Who?"

"Dawson, the man from the Pentagon. He said Oraschuk, who comes from Hamburg, was to accompany the crate to Frankfurt. Going home to visit her sick old mother. But the Soviet agents didn't like her. So they sent Dovosky instead."

"Lucky for her."

I shrugged. "She'll have plenty of time to think about luck in jail."

"Are you going to bring charges against Mrs. Beech and her son?"

"I've thought about it a great deal, and decided not to. She's lost her husband. That's punishment enough."

Marshall grunted. "Gilbertson let drop the fact that he heard Operation *Starlight* had been launched and is in operation."

"That gives us a three-year lead over the Russians." Then the spiral of new high-technology would take another upward twist: new emerging technology to improve the current outdated systems, and on and on ...

"How can I thank you for the part you played in all this?"

"You know I enjoyed myself." I fingered the spot on my head.

"Send your bill directly to me. I'll see that it's paid promptly."

"What shall I do about the jack?"

"What are you talking about?"

I told him. "But when I took it back to Hertz they denied it was theirs. Should I deduct it from my expense account?"

He chuckled. "What car do you drive?"

"A Mercedes. It won't fit."

"Perhaps you can use it for *Holy Ghost*."

We laughed. "By the way," he said, "I'm thinking of taking a vacation now this case is wrapped up. A fishing holiday out on the coast. D'you know any good spots?"

"I'll find out and fly you up in *Holy Ghost*. Pender keeps telling me I need a vacation. Make it soon."